Up Next:

Thea Stilton

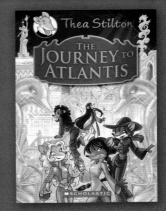

Secret Fairies

Don't miss any of these exciting series featuring the Thea Sisters!

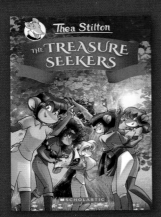

Treasure Seekers

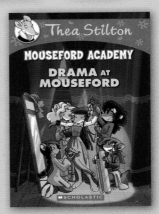

Mouseford Academy

Geronimo Stilton

ISLAND OF DRAGONS

THE TWELFTH ADVENTURE IN THE KINGDOM OF FANTASY

Scholastic Inc.

Published by Scholastic Inc., *Publishers since 1920*, 557 Broadway, New York, NY 10012. SCHOLASTIC and associated logos are trademarks and/or registered trademarks of Scholastic Inc.

Stilton is the name of a famous English cheese. It is a registered trademark of the Stilton Cheese Makers' Association. For more information, go to www.stiltoncheese.com.

This book is a work of fiction. Names, characters, places, and incidents are either the product of the author's imagination or are used fictitiously, and any resemblance to actual persons, living or dead, business establishments, events, or locales is entirely coincidental.

Library of Congress Cataloging-in-Publication Data available

ISBN 978-1-338-54693-4

Text by Geronimo Stilton
Original title *L'isola dei draghi*
Cover by Iacopo Bruno, Silvia Bigolin, Christian Aliprandi, and Mauro De Toffol
Illustrations by Silvia Bigolin, Ivan Bigarella, Alessandro Muscillo, and Christian Aliprandi
Graphics by Marta Lorini

Special thanks to Becky Herrick
Translated by Julia Heim
Interior design by Becky James

10 9 8 7 6 5 4 3 2 1   19 20 21 22 23

Printed in China   62

First edition, September 2019

DRAGONIA: THE ISLAND OF DRAGONS

My dear rodent readers, would you ever have guessed that I would bring you with me to Dragonia — the legendary Island of Dragons?

It's a truly enchanted place, full of amazing dragons who are known for their courage, their sincerity, their wisdom, their knowledge, and their wit! So, what are we waiting for? Let's go! It will be an adventure to make your tail *tremble*!

It all began on a warm morning in New Mouse City. The day's first rays of sunlight shone through my window and woke me up.

It was Sunday, the only day of the week that I didn't have to go into the office, and . . . Oh, excuse me! I haven't introduced myself. My name is Stilton, *Geronimo Stilton*, and I run *The Rodent's Gazette,* the most famouse newspaper on all of Mouse Island.

Anyway, as I was saying, that morning I turned over in my bed, enjoying my rest, when suddenly, a loud song started playing . . .

Hey there, mouse, are you looking at me?
I think you are sweeter than Brie!
Just like ricotta, my heart is mush,
Because you, lovely mouselet . . .
are my crush!

But . . . where was it coming from? The window was closed, the radio was off, and I was the only one home! Suddenly, I realized that the song was coming from . . . my **MousePhone**! I had forgotten that my nephew Benjamin had installed his favorite band's latest hit as my ringtone. Squeak!

I answered the phone, and the music finally stopped. "H-hello?"

A loud voice answered, "Hi, it's THEA! You aren't in bed, are you? Get up and get dressed! I need a favor."

A favor? **OH NO!** I just knew my sister would drag me into some sort of crazy escapade.

Thea continued, "I need you to take my place as tour guide!"

"A tour guide? For what?" I was totally confused!

Thea explained, "*Tremblina Noir*, the famouse

actress and star of many of Creepella's films, is visiting. I was supposed to take her on a tour of New Mouse City, but I still have some work to do. So I need you to take her around town! She'll be at your house in ten minutes."

"**TEN MINUTES?!**" I exclaimed. "**BUT I'M NOT READY!**"

"So hurry up!" Thea said. "Thanks, G! I'll call you later to see how it's going." *Click!*

Thea had hung up!

Holey cheese! There was no time to lose. In **ten minutes**, I had to get up, stretch, brush my teeth, take a shower, comb my whiskers, get dressed, eat breakfast, make the bed, fold my pajamas,

I had to stretch...

brush my teeth...

take a shower...

comb my whiskers...

make the bed . . .

fold my pajamas . . .

eat breakfast . . .

water the plants on the terrace, and . . .

ding-dong!

water the plants . . .

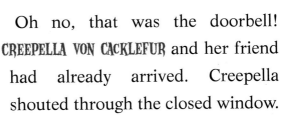

get dressed . . .

Oh no, that was the doorbell! CREEPELLA VON CACKLEFUR and her friend had already arrived. Creepella shouted through the closed window.

"Hurry up, lazyfur! Aren't you ready yet? Don't keep us waiting — come on!"

Moldy mozzarella, why did everything always happen to me?!

JUST TWO LITTLE THINGS!

I got dressed as quickly as my **PAWS** could carry me. Then I went downstairs and opened the front door.

"G-good morning!" I squeaked.

Instead of jumping to give me a huge **hug**, as she usually did, Creepella just stared at me.

Strange. Very strange. Very, very strange . . .

I said hello to her friend. "Y-you must be Miss Noir!"

The mouse gave me a strange look and said, "Nice to meet you."

Creepella swatted me with her **bag** and said, "My sweet little bat wing is always joking around. Right? Now go change!"

Change? Why? What was **wrong** with my suit?

I looked down at myself and . . . Oh noooo! I looked like such a CHEESEBRAIN! With all the rushing around, I had forgotten to change out of my pajama pants! FASTER than you could twitch a whisker, I ran up to my room to change and then came back down.

What a cheesebrain!

This time, Creepella leaped over to hug me.

"That's much better, Gerrykins! Oh, it's going to be a fangtastic Sunday!"

Finally, she took her PAWS off me, and I turned to her friend. "It's nice to meet you, Miss Noir! I know that you have been in many of Creepella's films."

Tremblina smiled. "You're such a gentlemouse! But there's no need to be so formal. And, of course, it's thanks to the talent of a director like

Creepella that I have won a **Screamy** and two Werewolf Hamster Awards in my career!"

Creepella shook her snout. "No, no, no! It's because of your acting! You were a scream in *The Ghost of Fang Villa*, and the **critics** are still raving about your character in *Attack of the Spirit Ship*."

But Tremblina insisted, "My dear mouse, thank you, really, but the **credit** is all *yours*!"

"And I say it's *yours*!"

"No, no, it's *yours*!"

Shopping!

I butted in. "Umm, excuse me, mouselets! Would you like to start touring the city? We could take a walk down to Singing Stone Square . . ."

Tremblina shook her head and said, "We want to go **shopping**! I just need to get

Huff . . .

two little things to freshen my wardrobe."

Shopping?! Thea hadn't said anything about shopping . . . But I couldn't back out now.

TEN pairs of shoes, **FIFTEEN** handbags, and **TWENTY** dresses later, Creepella and Tremblina were still dragging me to stores all over New Mouse City.

And guess who carried all the bags? I did!

Squeak!

Moldy mozzarella, why did everything always happen to me?!

"That's the last of it," Creepella said, putting another bag in my **PAW**.

I breathed a sigh of relief. "Is it

9

finally time to go?"

"Don't be **silly**, lazyfur!" Creepella responded. "We finished shopping, but we have to go to the Ratson Pollock exhibit: NINETY-THREE ROOMS. It's in the Museum of Modern Art with the rest of his most famouse works!"

CHEESE STICKS! Ninety-three rooms?!

Tremblina continued, "And then we'll go out to dinner at that restaurant with the fabumouse view of the city. It got a five-cheese ranking in the restaurant guide *The Gluttonous Mouse*!"

SIGH! I WAS ONE EXHAUSTED RODENT!

But I went along with them.

I was so tired that I almost fell **asleep** at the dinner table. When I jolted myself awake, I said, "My dearest mice, I believe it's time for bed!"

Tremblina burst out laughing. "Ha, ha, ha! Your friend is always joking around, Creepella.

Now let's go dancing!"

PAWS ON THE DANCE FLOOR!

Dancing?! I'm not exactly a club rat. Plus, I was tired — so tired — SO VERY TIRED!

Creepella said to me, "Come on, Gerry, don't be such a **PETRIFIED MUMMY**! You just need the right look."

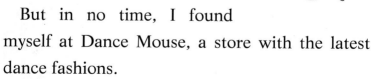

I'm soooo sleepy!

I yawned deeply and replied, "Wh-why? My suit is just fine!"

But in no time, I found myself at Dance Mouse, a store with the latest dance fashions.

Creepella and Tremblina shoved me into a dressing room and began passing me the strangest **clothes** I had ever seen . . .

"Try this one, my little **bat wing**!" Creepella suggested.

"This one, too!" Tremblina added.

Tango dancer

As I changed from one outfit to another, my sister, Thea, called. "Hi, G! Where are you?"

"At Dance Mouse . . ." I responded wearily.

Hip-hop dancer

"Good job, brother! You could stand to spruce up your look. Stay there. There's a **SURPRISE** coming your way!" *Click!*

Cheese niblets, what did that mean?!

Maybe she had finished with the **photos** for the

Russian folk dancer

Samba dancer

Flamenco dancer

Tap dancer

newspaper. Or maybe she was coming to save me. Maybe she would go dancing with Creepella and Tremblina!

The bell over the store door rang. I lifted my eyes and saw . . . my cousin **Trap**!

He entered and yelled, "Geronimooooooo! Thea told me that there are two lovely mouselets who could use a **real** tour guide . . ."

He put his arms around Creepella and Tremblina, and said, "Two fascinating mice like yourselves need a worthy companion! We're off to heat up the dance floor, little G.

The night is young!"

In a flash, I was alone, dressed like a FOOL!

Moldy mozzarella, why did everything always happen to me?!

As soon as I stuck my snout into the **dance hall**, Tremblina scurried over.

Ballet dancer

Rock 'n' roll dancer

What's wrong with this?

Seventies dancer

Ha, ha, ha!

"Finally, you're here! Creepella and your friendly cousin are already dancing. Let's show them what we're made of!"

I tried to tell Tremblina that I didn't know how to dance, but she just grabbed me and began to twirl.

I complained, "My head is sp-spinning . . ."

She said, "It's the excitement of dancing, Geronimo!"

Trap and Creepella danced right by us.

My cousin said, "Geronimo, are you dancing

Gerrykins!

or are you polishing the floors? Come on! Feel the rhythm in your paws!"

Creepella, on the other hand, squeaked, "Gerrykins!

I thought you said you couldn't dance!"

Then, with a spin, they disappeared into the crowd.

After a few songs, I was beyond tired.

Huff! Pant! "I'm sorry, Tremblina, I need to stop for a bit," I said.

In a corner of the room, I found a nice little couch. Ahh, how comfortable!

I was about to **nod off** . . . when Tremblina found me.

"Here's where you ended up! Come on, don't be **shy**, Geronimo. We still have all night to dance!"

Slimy Swiss cheese! **ALL NIGHT?!**

I started to say, "I'm sorry, but I am really tir —"

But I didn't finish

Don't be shy!

my sentence, because Tremblina had grabbed my **PAW** and was dragging me back onto the dance floor.

"You need to loosen up!" she said. "Feel the music in your fur!"

I tried to go sit down, but Tremblina was **holding** me so tight that I couldn't. Creepella passed and exclaimed, "Gerrykins, dance with **MEEEEE!**"

Feel the music!

But she disappeared before I could respond.

Then an even faster song started. Tremblina and I began to twirl and twirl and twirl . . .

I squeaked, "Heeeelp! My head is spinning . . ."

But that mouse was unstoppable. "Follow the beat, my dear! Let yourself go!"

My head was spinning so much that I felt sick. I closed my eyes, but that made it worse: I felt like I was flying! **Heeeelp!**

In the Kingdom of Fantasy

When I opened my eyes, I really *was* flying! I was seated on the back of a strong, majestic

DRAGON!

Well, actually, I wasn't really seated — it was more like I was clinging on for dear life because we were so high in the air. Squeak! I don't like heights — I'm too fond of my fur! How did I get here?

The dragon reassured me. "Don't worry, Knight! We are almost there!"

Just then, from between the clouds, I could see a sparkling palace in the shape of a giant fLOWeR.

As soon as the dragon dropped me off at the

LOTUS'S DRAGON
The King and Queen of Lotus Flowers sent their court dragon to go get Sir Geronimo of Stilton, the fearless knight.

entrance to the palace, I ran into an elf with pointed ears. He grabbed my paw and cried,

"SIR GERONIMO OF STILTON!

You're finally here! My name is Alyssum — I'm the court page."

I said hello in return, then asked, "Umm . . . Where are we?"

"We are in the *Kingdom of Lotus Flowers*," the elf responded. "It is one of the farthest territories on the border of the Kingdom of Fantasy. It is a magnificent place, populated by kind creatures who love **nature**."

I looked around at the palace's garden, and it was clear that the inhabitants of this kingdom loved nature very much and took great care of it.

I said, "I've never heard of this kingdom in all my travels. Can you tell me why I'm here?"

"The KING AND QUEEN OF LOTUS FLOWERS will explain everything to you," the elf said. "Come, I will introduce you!"

He led me to

the main room of the MAJESTIC palace. At its center, seated on two flower-shaped thrones, the king and the queen greeted us with a kind hello. The king stood up to meet us while the elf made the introductions.

"Fearless knight, this is King Lotus and Queen Lily."

I knelt down and said, "It is an HONOR to meet you!"

Queen Lily smiled, but she seemed quite sad. King Lotus grabbed my paw and said seriously, "We have heard so much about you. Thank you for being here, Guardian!"

I responded, "Um, you're welcome? I haven't done anything yet!"

But before he could squeak again, I looked up in shock — at the end of the room I saw many of my friends from the

KINGDOM OF FANTASY.

And Blossom, Queen of the Fairies, was there!

I hugged them all one by one. "How nice to see you, **my friends**! Is there some sort of party?!" I exclaimed.

But there was worry on all their faces. This time, something **REALLY SERIOUS** must have happened. Just my luck.

We need your help, Knight!

What happened?

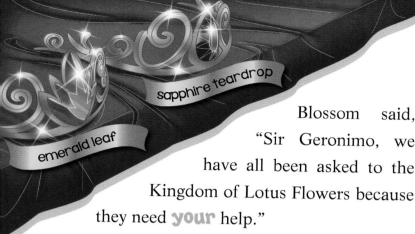

emerald leaf

sapphire teardrop

Blossom said, "Sir Geronimo, we have all been asked to the Kingdom of Lotus Flowers because they need **your** help."

Queen Lily sighed and said, "Our five daughters have been kidnapped!"

Great Gouda!

FIVE PRINCESSES HAD BEEN KIDNAPPED?!

Blossom said, "The princesses were in the garden when they suddenly disappeared."

"It was the terrible witch **Darkrock**, the mistress of Sorrowstone Castle," Alyssum added. "It's a very gloomy place, where everything is made of stone — even the clouds!"

Cheese niblets, how scary! My paws went as **limp** as string cheese just thinking about it.

Blossom said to me, "Knight, look!" And she opened a chest that was on a crystal dresser. In the chest were five CROWNS. They were all shaped differently, and each one had a decoration in the center made of a precious gem. There was:

an emerald leaf,

a sapphire teardrop,

a diamond edelweiss flower,

an opal dragonfly,

and an amber head of wheat.

diamond edelweiss

opal dragonfly

amber wheat

Queen Lily explained, "These crowns belong to our daughters. Each represents a part of the *beauty* of nature that we care for. A **STONE MONSTER** brought them to us with a message from the witch . . ."

I stammered, "Wh-what did th-the message say?"

"Come get your princesses,
if you dare!"

Blossom responded.

Then Scribblehopper cleared his throat and croaked, "**Your Majesty**, I actually think the note said something more like this: '*If the damsels you wish to save, my brutal power you must brave!*'"

Leave it to Scribblehopper

to turn a threat into a bad poem. Then I realized what he'd said. "Um . . . what **BRUTAL POWER** are you talking about?" I asked.

Queen Lily said, "Darkrock has the power to transform everything to **STONE**. That's why the princesses are in great DANGER and we need to save them as fast as possible!"

"Wh-who would dare go to SORROWSTONE CASTLE?" I said.

A light of hope shone in the **EYES** of the king and queen. "You, Knight!

I responded, "But I'm not a knight!"

Then Queen Lily approached a large wardrobe and opened it: Inside there was a sparkling set of armor.

King Lotus said, "Of course you are! This is for you, Knight!"

THE ANCIENT PROPHECY
OF DRAGONIA

After putting on the **armor**, I stammered, "Queen Lily, I — I would v-very much like to help, but I'm n-not as courageous as you think! I'm actually quite a scaredy-mouse!"

The Queen of Lotus Flowers put a hand on my arm and looked me in the eyes. "Knight, *we have faith in you,* and you should have some in yourself," she said. "You are the knight who will save us. My **heart** tells me so, and above all, so does:

THE PROPHECY
OF DRAGONIA!"

The Prophecy of Dragonia?! Cheese sticks, what was that?

I responded, "There must be a mistake. I don't even know what **Dragonia** is!"

"Come with me, Knight," Queen Lily said. Then she gestured to Blossom and King Lotus, and led us out of the *palace*. Scribblehopper, King Chuckles, Factual, Cozy, and Mixy followed. We walked and walked. I sure was out of shape!

We crossed some woods and went over a small lake. Huff! Puff! Pant!

We went down a stone path and crossed a swamp. Huff! Puff! Pant!

We went over a field and headed down another path. Huff! Puff! Pant!

Finally, we arrived in a clearing where there was a tiny wooden house with a **minuscule** door. We managed to all slip through it into a dusty room. In the middle of the room, on a worn WOODEN stand, there was an ancient-looking **scroll**. It was so old and faded that you almost couldn't read what was written on it.

Queen Lily announced, "Here is the ancient **PROPHECY OF DRAGONIA**! It has been held in the Kingdom of Lotus Flowers for centuries."

I squinted at the words to see better and read the scroll . . .

Mother of all mice! Was I really the knight it was referring to?! That couldn't be. I took a pawstep closer to the scroll's stand, but something jumped in front of me. Something **GREEN**. What was happening?! In front of me was . . . *a tower of pixies!*

"Get your paws off that paper!" yelled the pixie at the top of the tower.

Queen Lily intervened. "Stay calm, friends. He is the **KNIGHT** from the legend!"

THE PROPHECY OF DRAGONIA

An evil witch, one terrible day,
will steal all peace and harmony away.
Five princesses will by her be taken,
and in her evil realm, they'll
remain forsaken.

They can only be set free by
one fearless knight
with five great dragons to help
him win the fight.

Each dragon with a special quality,
which the fearless knight will clearly see!
To the island of dragons he must go
and find the creatures that he will know:
one whose courage is the very best,
one who's most sincere and honest,
one whose wisdom tops the chart,
one who's silly — but also quite smart,
and one who's happy, with the
greatest wit.
That shouldn't be a problem, should it?

Water Dragons

Forest Dragons

The Pixies chattered among themselves.

"He *is*?"

"Really, **HE'S** the one?"

"But he's so skinny — so delicate — so MUSHY!"

"Well, er . . ." I tried to respond.

The queen said, "These are the Herald Pixies. Their people have always watched over the Prophecy of Dragonia scroll."

Finally, I asked, "Can someone tell me what Dragonia is?!"

"IT'S THE ISLAND OF DRAGONS!"

the Queen explained. "It is home to five kingdoms, populated by five species of dragon who each have a particular gift.

"The **FOREST DRAGONS** are known for their courage,

the **WATER DRAGONS** for their sincerity,

the MOUNTAIN DRAGONS for their wisdom,

the **SWAMP DRAGONS** for their intelligence, and

the FIELD DRAGONS for their humor."

Mountain Dragons

Swamp Dragons

Field Dragons

King Lotus added, "There is a great and ancient **friendship** between our kingdom and Dragonia, because the first king of Lotus Flowers learned how to love **NATURE** from the dragons.

"From that point on, we have done our best to take care of the natural *beauty* that surrounds us, just as the dragons do."

Blossom concluded, "Knight, you need to explore **Dragonia** and find the dragons from the prophecy. Then you leave for SORROWSTONE CASTLE. But I am sure that you will find the dragons you need!"

My friends said to me in unison, "You can do it, Knight!"

They always managed to reassure me with their affection. Even though I was scared stiff, I knew that I couldn't leave the princesses in the claws of an EVIL WITCH!

I took a deep breath. "As you wish, my queen! I will go to Dragonia. Who is coming with me?"

Blossom responded, "The prophecy speaks OF ONLY ONE KNIGHT! So, for the mission to be successful, you'll need to go on your own!"

GIFTS . . . LOTS OF GIFTS

I had to go alone?! My whiskers *drooped*, and I complained. "Those dragons will roast me! I'll be made into **mouse meatballs** before I even meet the terrifying witch Darkrock!"

Blossom tried to cheer me up. "Have courage, Knight! We will help you. We brought you some **GIFTS**! So, even if we are far away, you will have something to remind you of us, and you won't feel so alone."

SCRIBBLEHOPPER was the first to give me his gift: It was a large, heavy **B O O K**, with what seemed like an infinite number of pages!

A book for you!

My frog friend said proudly, "Sir Geronimo, I know just how much you will miss me. That's why I've decided to give you this *poetry collection — written by me!*"

I opened a page randomly and read the title aloud: *"The Song of the Squid Sighing on a Stone at Sunset."*

Scribblehopper exclaimed, "Oh, that's one of my **favorites**!"

Yikes, that poem sounded like a real **snooze-fest**! It did not give me much hope for the others . . .

But I didn't want to disappoint him, so I said, "I will be happy to read them. Thanks!"

Then it was Chuckles's turn. He gave me a tiny **flute**. It was so small that it fit on the tip of my paw!

Then **Mixy**, the troll chef who now lives with the gnomes, stepped forward and gave me a big basket.

Mixy said, "Dear Knight, let me present you with my specialty:

SHORTBREAD SWIRL!"

When I opened the basket, the stench of onion, **rotten** food, and troll toots curled my fur. Putrid Parmesan, how awful!

Mixy continued, "It is the most **nutritious** cookie there is! Take it with you and you'll never be hungry."

It was, in fact, an enormouse cookie . . . but it did not look at all **appetizing**.

SHORTBREAD SWIRL!

If it's shortbread swirl you want to make
this ancient recipe is what you should bake:
Just a few ingredients, but they're unique,
and it's so good it'll make you shriek!

INGREDIENTS:

- Fermented garlic aged inside a witch's shoe
- Werewolf snot marinated in slug drool
- Chopped-up troll scabs
- Onion juice strained through the wrinkles of a thousand-year-old tortoise

Mix all the ingredients until they form a dough, then knead it for three days and three nights. Roll out the dough into a large cookie shape, cook it on low heat, and it will be ready in no time!

When she listed the ingredients, I became as PALE as mozzarella!

The troll chef added, "I'm **warning** you, don't finish it all at once! Just eat a little piece at a time, or it won't last you throughout the trip."

As I tried not to faint from the STENCH, I responded, "I will try not to . . . um . . . eat it too quickly. Thanks, Mixy!"

My friends were really generous! Now I had all these gifts, but there was one problem! I didn't have any place to put them . . .

Factual and Cozy came to my rescue. The King of Gnomes said to me, "A fearless knight can't travel with such a load! That's why we brought you a **BOTTOMLESS BAG** to carry all your gifts in." Then Factual handed me a tiny, tiny bag . . .

I thanked him. "What a wonderful gift! But I think it's a bit small to carry everything . . ."

That made the King of Gnomes **burst out laughing**. "Ha, ha, ha! Don't be fooled by appearances! This bag is special: It could even hold a whole **dragon**!"

And to prove it, he asked for each of the **GIFTS** I had received, and one by one he fit them all in!

I was in disbelief. "**HOW** did you do that?! And **WHERE** did all my things go?!"

Factual smiled and responded, "Take a look!"

He stuck his hand in the bag and fished out all the gifts again as I watched in **amazement**.

"How fabumouse!" I exclaimed. "Thanks!" And I put the

Ack!

This is for you!

book, the flute, and the cookie back in.

Blossom approached. "KNIGHT, I also have a gift for you," she said. Then she bent down and gave me a kiss on the forehead. My whiskers trembled with emotion!

The Queen of the Fairies said, "This kiss contains all the LOVE we have for you. It will give you courage when you need it."

Now the moment of departure had almost arrived. But the King and Queen of Lotus Flowers had one last GIFT reserved for me.

Lily took the scroll with the prophecy on it and gave it to me. "Take this, Knight. It will guide you along your journey!"

My whiskers trembled with feeling again. "Thanks, Queen Lily, King Lotus!" I said.

Everyone gathered around the palace entrance, where the Lotus Flower court dragon was waiting.

Queen Lily explained, "My trusted friend will take you to faraway Dragonia. Now hurry, Knight . . . Every minute is precious for the princesses. Good luck!"

"Good luck!" called everyone together.

Blossom smiled and said, "Knight, come back with the princesses! We will be waiting eagerly!"

I tried to be a brave mouse, though my insides were churning. I promised solemnly, "I will not disappoint you. MOUSE'S HONOR!"

I climbed onto the court dragon's back and said good-bye to everyone. But as we lifted off in FLIGHT and headed toward the mysterious Island of Dragons, I could only think of one thing:

HOLEY CHEESE, I WAS SO SCARED!

KINGDOM OF THE
FIELD DRAGONS

KINGDOM OF THE
SWAMP DRAGONS

KINGDOM OF THE
WATER DRAGONS

DRAGONIA: THE ISLAND OF DRAGONS

KINGDOM OF THE MOUNTAIN DRAGONS

KINGDOM OF THE FOREST DRAGONS

So Terribly Alone!

We traveled for a long time, flying over the many lands of the KINGDOM OF FANTASY. I was so terrified! Who knew what was waiting for me in Dragonia?! What if the dragons had BAD attitudes? What if their favorite dish was **roasted mouse**? What if —

Suddenly, Dragonia appeared in the middle of the sea: It was shaped like . . .

a giant dragon!

The court dragon took a scenic route down. "Enjoy the landscape, Knight!" he said.

From above, the island seemed like a palette of colors: the GREEN of the woods, the WHITE of the mountains, the YELLOW of the grain fields . . . what a mousetastically beautiful landscape!

We landed on a clearing near the coast. The trip had been **so long** that when I got off the dragon's back, my tail was sore.

My dragon friend said good-bye, rubbing his snout against my armor and **singing**, *"I'm sorry I can't come with you, but I'm sure you'll make it through!"*

I whimpered, "I wish I were as sure as you are!"

Then the court dragon took off, back to the Kingdom of Lotus Flowers. I stood there watching him fly away, and soon he was just a tiny sparkle in the sky. I felt awful. I was . . .

ALONE,
SO ALONE,
SO TERRIBLY ALONE

in a new, unknown land! Squeak!

Right then, I felt a PiñCh on my tail . . .

I looked around quickly, but I didn't see anyone.

"Wh-who's there?" I stammered.

"It's me! I'm here, Knight!" a small voice said.

I stood still. Where was that coming from?

A moment later I felt another PiñCh on my tail . . .

"I'm right here. Can't you see me?"

At that moment, something FLASHED before my eyes and landed near my paws.

"Hello, Knight! My name is Jasmine, but everyone calls me Jazzy!" Before me was a small pixie! She looked cheerful and clever.

I looked at her, stunned. "Hey! **WHERE** did you come from? **WHat** are you doing here?!"

She began to jump and twirl in the air. "You didn't realize, but I traveled with you from the Kingdom of Lotus Flowers! I was hiding behind

Jazzy the Pixie

An adventurous and resourceful pixie, Jazzy has always dreamed of going off on exciting journeys in search of faraway kingdoms. She is easily bored and loves getting into trouble, but she is also very skilled at finding solutions to her friends' problems. There are two things of hers you can't touch: her family and the portrait she always carries with her, which is rolled up in a cylinder that she keeps in her hat!

you on the dragon! I want to travel and live through a thousand adventures and be a hero! Move over, **monsters**! Shoo, **WITCHES**! Watch out, trolls, you ugly —"

"Hey, j-just a moment!" I interrupted. "You can't come with me. The prophecy says that only **one** knight can go on the mission!"

Jazzy shook her head and said, "The prophecy says '**one fearless knight**,' not '**one knight alone**'! And even if you don't seem very fearless, the only knight here is you. So, I can come, too. I will be your helper!"

Then she pulled from her hat a slingshot made with a nutshell and a blade of grass. She loaded it and aimed it here and there right and left, up and down!

"Where are you, enemy? Get ready for Jazzy, you softies! Show your snouts, you fools!"

Cheesecake! I had the feeling that this PiXiE was going to get me into loads of trouble!

Moldy mozzarella, why does everything always happen to me?!

I headed into the woods, trying to discourage her. "Your parents will be worried! It's better if you go hoooooome . . ."

I WAS FAAAAALLLINGGGGG!!

I ended up hanging on to the edge of a hole that was **super deep and truly enormouse**!

It had been hidden by branches. But now I couldn't get out!

A Pixie for a Friend

J azzy leaped into action in a flash of green and extended a willow branch to me.

"GRAB ON, KNIGHT!" she called.

I managed to grab on to the branch and pull myself up to safety.

Heeelp!

I thanked the pixie profusely. "Thank you . . . **Pant!** . . . Jazzy! You . . . **Huff! Pant!** . . . saved me!"

She gave me a confused look, and said, "You sure do have a talent for getting into trouble!"

Now I was confused. "What are you talking about?"

"You have a **CHESTNUT BURR** stuck on your snout!" she responded, laughing even more.

CRUSTY CHEDDAR! I was a total mess.

I pulled off the burr (*ouch!*), brushed the **leaves** off my armor, and tried to act like a fearless knight.

Jazzy said to me, "You are a bit **CLUMSY**, but I hear you are the greatest **hero**

Crusty cheddar!

of the Kingdom of Fantasy. So, can I come with you?"

I responded, "Yes, okay! You can come with me!" In the end I was **happy** to have company. Plus, Jazzy was right: She wasn't a knight, so she wouldn't affect the prophecy.

The pixie began to jump around. "Hooray! YIPPEE! Let's go! Mom and Dad will be so proud! Wait, I'll show them to you . . ."

She fished a small WOODEN CYLINDER out of her hat, opened it, and pulled out a rolled-up piece of paper.

"This is a portrait of my family! I always carry it with me," she said.

Cheese niblets! Jazzy sure had a big family!

Between **jumps**, Jazzy explained, "The portrait was made for my great-great-great-great-grandfather Tristan's **three hundredth birthday**." She pointed to the elderly pixie in the middle of the portrait: He had the longest beard!

Jazzy continued, "This is my uncle Glutton with Grandma Snicker. This is my cousin Firlywhirl and my beloved aunt Golly with the twins Tick and Tack. Then over here is my dear cousin Twirly with Uncle Harry, and here . . ."

One by one, Jazzy, pointed out who each of the **thousand** pixies in the portrait were, but I couldn't keep up. My head was spinning!

That pixie was so lively!

GAME
Pixies love acorns and
nuts! How many acorns
and nuts are in this
family portrait?

"**How exciting!**" Jazzy cried. "Are there going to be dangerous animals in the forest? Biting spiders, I'll break their legs! **Poisonous snakes**, I'll tie them in knots!"

We were in the woods now, and as we moved forward, the trees got taller and taller. They were really tall — so very tall — unfathomably tall! In fact, they were as tall as a

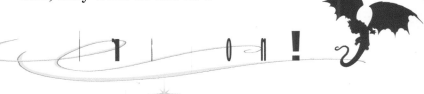

We were entering the

KINGDOM OF THE Forest Dragons.

THE FOREST DRAGONS

We found ourselves in the biggest and lushest forest I had ever seen. There were mushrooms as big as trees growing in the underbrush — and the trees were as tall as skyscrapers. I felt as tiny as a fly. But it actually wasn't scary — it was relaxing! There was a *lovely scent* of leaves and moss.

I said to Jazzy, "It's so peaceful! Listen to the calm of the forest, the rustling of the leaves, nature's easy quiet . . ."

ROOAAAARRR!

An earsplitting roar thundered through the air. I looked up . . . and found myself snout to snout with A DRAGON!

She landed in front of me, opened her mouth wide . . . and said, "**Oh, excuse me!** Did I scare you?"

Did I scare you?

So she didn't want to eat me?! **HOLEY CHEESE**, what a relief!

I stammered, "Umm . . . j-just a bit . . ."

She bared her **FANGS** once more (was that a smile?) and exclaimed, "You're the **fearless knight**, right?!"

Jazzy responded, "Yes, it's the knight — it's him in the **FUR AND WHISKERS**! And I'm Jazzy, his helper."

The dragon introduced herself, extending her paw. **"My name is Maple."**

I shook her paw. "Nice to . . . **aaack**!"

Though she actually wasn't that big, she was really **STRONG**!

Maple continued, "It's an honor to meet you! **King Baobab** will be so happy to have you with us. Come, I will take you to his palace!"

"Will you take me . . . by flying?" I gulped, pale as mozzarella.

"Of course!" Maple said. "We live in the tops of the **trees**."

Rancid ricotta! More flying? I didn't know how I would survive my visit.

But I thought of my **MISSION** and of the missing princesses. I had to find them!

Jazzy and I climbed onto the dragon's back, and she darted up toward the tops of the trees.

Jazzy was very enthusiastic. "**Yippee!** How marvelous! Look how high up we are!"

I, on the other hand, kept my eyes closed and was grabbing on to Maple's neck for dear life. My fur was **trembling** with fear!

We soon landed on a platform in front of

BAOBAB'S PALACE,

and the king came out to meet us.

"Welcome to the Kingdom of the Forest Dragons!" he said.

He shook — or, should I say, **squashed** — my paw and said, "Knight, we have heard much about you. What brings you to our land?"

I bowed and explained, "I am on a mission on behalf of the people of Lotus Flowers. I'm here to find the most **COURAGEOUS** dragon in Dragonia to help save the king and queen's five daughters. They have been kidnapped!"

Then I began reading him the prophecy **scroll**. King Baobab grumbled, embarrassed. "Oh, of course, of course . . . the **PROPHECY** . . . But now, what do you say to a **Banquet**?"

Strange! He had cut the prophecy short and seemed almost uncomfortable. For the king of the most courageous dragons of Dragonia, he didn't seem very enthusiastic about the mission . . .

The king clapped his paws and called, "Spoonilla! Beanie! Tell the cook to prepare an especially **grand** lunch!"

Then he turned toward us. "While we wait, I will show you our kingdom," he said. "Our city is suspended in the trees, and all the buildings are linked by a **SERIES OF BRIDGES.**

In front of you is the **Beech Bookworm School** and

next to it is the **Silent Oak Library**. Over there is the Happy Poppy Playground for the little ones, and the *BLAZING MUSHROOM GRILL* for those with refined palates."

I noticed an area that looked like a gym, but it was all covered with dust and SPIDERWEBS.

"It seems like no one has used that gym in a while!" I said.

Baobab, embarrassed, immediately changed the subject . . .

There was no doubt:

THE KING WAS HIDING SOMETHING!

HELP! THE SCROUNGERS!

We sat down at an enormouse table with the dragons. My mouth immediately started watering: They had really prepared a whisker-licking-good feast!

Jazzy shrieked, "This is even grander than the banquet at my great-great-great-great-grandfather Tristan's birthday!"

It was all so delicious! I cleared my throat and said, "Thank you,

Shh . . . keep quiet!

everyone, for such a fabumouse welcome!"

The dragons immediately went silent, then smiled at me and resumed talking. But they were all talking quietly . . .

Strange! It's like they were afraid of being heard by someone . . .

Delicious!

Can I have a bit more blueberry sauce?

Psst . . . can you pass the salt?

Suddenly, in the distance, I heard a

GRUNT GRUNT,

ꞁꞁ ꞁ ꞁ ꞁ ꞁ ꞁ ꞁ

slurp slurp.

The dragons looked at one another, alarmed.

"Oh no!"

"Them again?"

"Help!"

"The Scroungers!"

I looked in the sky and saw a group of dragons
flying over our heads. They were all singing at the
top of their lungs, completely out of tune . . .

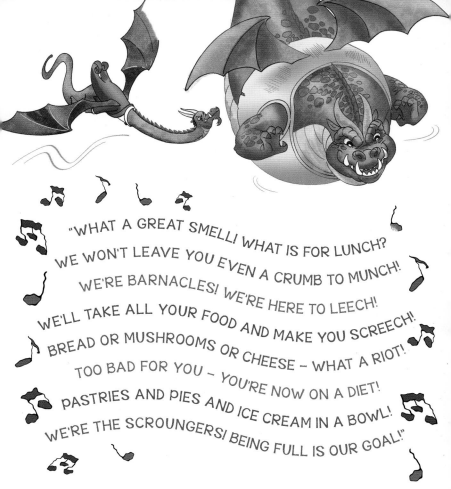

"WHAT A GREAT SMELL! WHAT IS FOR LUNCH?
WE WON'T LEAVE YOU EVEN A CRUMB TO MUNCH!
WE'RE BARNACLES! WE'RE HERE TO LEECH!
WE'LL TAKE ALL YOUR FOOD AND MAKE YOU SCREECH!
BREAD OR MUSHROOMS OR CHEESE – WHAT A RIOT!
TOO BAD FOR YOU – YOU'RE NOW ON A DIET!
PASTRIES AND PIES AND ICE CREAM IN A BOWL!
WE'RE THE SCROUNGERS! BEING FULL IS OUR GOAL!"

They landed with their paws on the table, getting mud everywhere.

The **BIGGEST** dragon, who must have been their leader, thundered, "Well, is that all? This is just an appetizer — where's the rest? Now we're

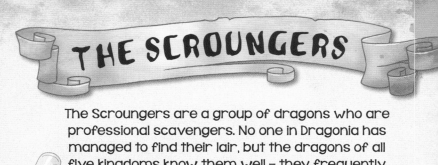

THE SCROUNGERS

The Scroungers are a group of dragons who are professional scavengers. No one in Dragonia has managed to find their lair, but the dragons of all five kingdoms know them well – they frequently come on raids and steal all the delights of any banquet, party, breakfast, lunch, dinner, or even snack that is taking place!

Gargantus

He is the leader of the gang and the worst scrounger of all. He can sniff out a banquet from an incredible distance. His motto is "You cook, I eat!"

Fillmeup

Don't be fooled by appearances: Even though he's as skinny as a rail, he is as voracious as a shark!

The Twins, Burp and Burble

They are inseparable troublemakers who always fight for the last mouthful.

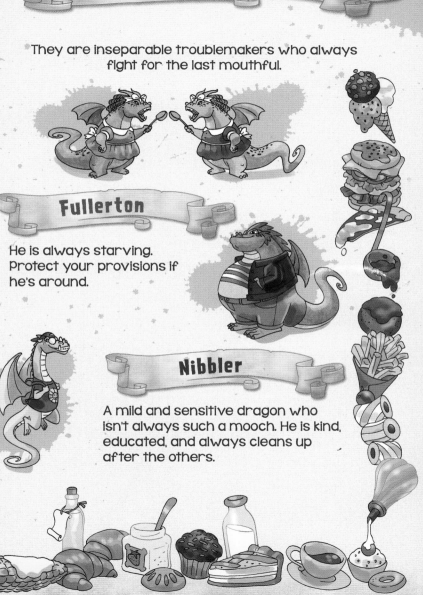

Fullerton

He is always starving. Protect your provisions if he's around.

Nibbler

A mild and sensitive dragon who isn't always such a mooch. He is kind, educated, and always cleans up after the others.

really **hungry**! And you know we always get what we want!"

"You're right, Gargantus! But this time, we'll let it go . . ." said another, very skinny dragon who was wearing a suit jacket.

A dragon who was smaller than the others and had glasses, braces on his teeth, and a backpack, muttered, "Excuse our disturbance . . . Sorry."

Two twin dragons, who had food splattered all over their clothes, laughed nastily at him. "Nibbler, you're such a wimp! Why don't you let loose and have some fun?"

The boss dragon roared, "STOP ALL THE CHATTERING! IT'S TIME TO CHOW DOWN!"

At that, the Scroungers all jumped into the banquet and gobbled everything up, faster than you could twitch a whisker!

Jazzy's face went from **green** to tomato **RED**. "I'll fix you, you dirty Scroungers! You're about to get a taste of my slingshot!"

But the Forest Dragons didn't react at all!

STRANGE! What had happened to their courage?

I approached King Baobab and asked, "Why do you let these **bullies** treat you like this?"

King Baobab sighed, **uncomfortable**. "They've been swooping in and eating everything in sight for years. We tried to S+◎P them, but it's never worked, and eventually we just gave up trying to resist . . ."

So that's what the king had been **hiding** from me: The Forest Dragons had stopped defending themselves. They had lost all of the **COURAGE** they once had.

But wasn't I the greatest expert on fear in the universe?

I will help you!

I had to help them!

A COURAGEOUS DRAGON!

Meanwhile, the Scroungers had finished gobbling everything down, leaving a disaster in their wake: **STAINS**, spilled drinks, and scraps of food.

What a feast!

They were flopped over the chairs, all burping in satisfaction and massaging their super-full bellies.

"I'm stuffed!"

"My gut is groaning!"

"My belly is about to burst!"

All of them, that is, but one.

The young dragon with glasses was very busy cleaning and tidying up the **MESS** the others had made.

Gargantus yelled, "Hey, Nibbler! If you want to clean up so badly, why don't you iron all the Forest Dragons' underwear while you're at it?"

All the Scroungers burst out laughing.

Nibbler turned as red as a pepper. It seemed like he had nothing in common with these other scoundrels. The **FOREST DRAGONS**, meanwhile, were in a corner watching everything in silence.

Then Gargantus said, "Now that we're full, let's go **digest** somewhere else. Go pack up the rest of the food. And I don't want any complaining during the trip!"

WHAT?! I was too scared to go up against these nasty dragons alone, but if anything ruffles my fur, it's **ARROGANCE**.

I said to the Forest Dragons, "Can't you do anything? They have **NO RIGHT** to act like this!"

Maple answered, "You're right, Knight!"

Fullerton heard me and yelled, "I'd concentrate

on saving your own fur if I were you!"

Meanwhile, Sycamore, the Forest Dragon cook, went to the kitchen and came back with a huge bag of provisions. Fillmeup grabbed it without a fuss, and the Scroungers started to head off, snickering along the way.

Before he left, Gargantus called, "Next time, put more chocolate on the cake!"

"THAT'S ENOUGH!" a voice thundered.

The Scroungers stopped suddenly, and all the Forest Dragons looked up.

Maple was the one who had spoken. She had blocked the Scroungers' path, and now stared at them fearlessly.

Gargantus tried making fun of her. "Oooh, I'm sooo scared! My paws are just trembling!"

But Maple wouldn't be intimidated. "We are tired of this! You have taken advantage of our hospitality."

Jazzy encouraged her. "Yeah! That's right! Tell 'em, Maple!"

Maple continued, "You won't come here to stuff yourselves anymore. We are the Forest Dragons . . . **and we won't allow it**!"

Gargantus realized that this dragon was serious. Suddenly, he lost his swagger and began backing down the walkway, quiet as a mouse. But Maple was superspeedy: She lifted off in flight, took the ropes that held up the walkway, and began to twirl and twirl and twirl them around.

Before he could even yell "Hey!" Gargantus found himself all tied up, as stuck as a rat in a trap.

"Well done, Maple!" Jazzy and I cheered.

I jumped for joy — and then realized I was on a THIN ROPE BRIDGE hanging in the sky. Jazzy and I nearly fell off!

The other Scroungers tried to escape, but the Forest Dragons made sure they got tied up as well. In a flash, those five gluttons were all **TRAPPED** in the walkway ropes.

Nibbler, who had stayed behind to clean up, looked at the scene with a gaping jaw. He didn't know what to say.

The Scroungers complained, "Untie us! We won't bother you again! **NEVER, EVER, EVER AGAIN!**"

Maple asked, "Are you sure?"

Gargantus, the biggest and greediest of all, whimpered, "Waaaah! We promise — just let us go!"

Maple exchanged glances with the other Forest Dragons, then agreed. "Oh, all right — we'll let you go."

With a sweep of her tail, she untwisted the walkways.

SWISSSSH!

The Scroungers darted off into the sky and disappeared . . .

The Forest Dragons were triumphant. They cheered for Maple:

"Hooray for Maple!"

King Baobab was moved, and exclaimed, "Let's get another BANQUET ready!"

Sycamore, the cook, answered, "Luckily we still have some things in the pantry!"

The Forest Dragons had rediscovered their lost courage, and I had found . . .

THE FIRST DRAGON FROM THE PROPHECY.

I exclaimed, "Maple, you are the most courageous dragon! Will you join us on our mission?"

She replied, "Of course!"

TRAVELING WITH NIBBLER

S ycamore prepared a fabumouse banquet to celebrate the victory over those nasty, freeloading Scroungers.

Surprisingly, Nibbler was there! Those cheesebrain Scroungers had left him behind.

"I'm GLAD you stayed," I said to him. "Those Scroungers just made fun of you and treated you badly."

Nibbler seemed to have regained his courage as well, and he smiled radiantly, putting his BRACES on display.

He explained, "I never fit in with the Scroungers, and I really think what they do is wrong. So thank you, Knight! Thanks to all of you!"

Then Jazzy — who, despite her tiny size, ate

as much as a dragon — offered him a piece of

raspberry cake.

"Do you want some, Nibbler?"

The dragon shook his head. "No, thank you. I've eaten enough!"

Great Gouda! He was such a polite dragon!

Want some cake?

No, thank you!

I asked, "What will you do now?"

Nibbler looked at the sky dreamily. "I don't know yet," he said. "I would like to travel. I would like to travel the world and help those who are less norfunate . . . fornutate . . . torfun . . ."

Jazzy gave him a gentle thump on the back.

"Fortunate!" he concluded. "Thanks, Jazzy!"

She smiled and said, "No worries!"

That dragon had a heart as soft as fondue!

"Why don't you join us?" I asked.

He jumped up from his chair happily. "Me?! You mean *me*? You want me with you, Knight?"

"Of course!" I said. "You seem like a dragon with STRONG paws on his legs. You could help us in a lot of ways. It would be nice to travel together!"

Nibbler turned RED all the way down to his tail:

He wasn't used to getting compliments!

"Hooray, hooray, hooray!" Jazzy cheered. "The more the merrier!"

Maple smiled — **Squeak!** I didn't know if I'd ever get used to her fangs! — and said, "It seems like it's time to go!"

SIGH!

She was right — but we'd just started to really get to know the Forest Dragons!

King Baobab clapped his paws to get everyone's attention.

CLAP! CLAP! CLAP!

Then he stood up and said, "Fearless Knight, without your help, we would never have regained our COURAGE. It is with great pride that I wish good luck to you and to our beloved Maple!"

And he sat back down with a thud.

"Oof!" he grumbled. "I'm not used to **feasts** like that anymore. Beanie, Spoonilla! Have the drago-llyptical dusted off at once! I will most definitely need it."

I smiled and responded, "It was my duty as Knight, King Baobab. I'm happy to have helped!"

Jazzy, Maple, Nibbler, and I gave everyone a hug, said good-bye, and prepared to leave. We were the start of Team Dragonia!

THE START OF TEAM DRAGONIA!

THE WATER DRAGONS

To reach the Kingdom of the Water Dragons, Maple convinced me to *fly* on her back. Rancid ricotta! I was not happy about it!

Jazzy, however, was having tons of fun flying with Nibbler. "Flying pixie, incomiiiiing!" she screeched as they swooped through the sky.

The air began to **smell** of algae and salt. Soon we saw a large stretch of blue before us, framed by rocks.

Maple announced, "Here we are:

THE KINGDOM OF THE WATER DRAGONS."

Jazzy squinted and said, "All I can see is water. Where are the dragons?"

"They live **under** the water," Maple explained.

Soon we landed on the seashore. "Are you ready to jump in?" Maple asked.

"Holey cheese — jump in?!" I cried. "How will we **breathe** underwater? What if a shark eats me? And what if —"

Maple interrupted me. "These waters are **enchanted**, Knight, just like everything in the Kingdom of Fantasy! You'll be able to breathe without gills. Have courage! On the count of three, we'll **jump in** together. One, two . . ."

"Wait!" Jazzy exclaimed. She pulled the container with the **portrait** of her family out of her hat. "I want to make sure that it's sealed up. If the portrait gets **WET**, it will get ruined!"

She twisted the cap, then said, "Ready!"

"And three!" Maple finished.

Jazzy dove lightly into the water.

 **PLINK!**

Maple went under, making an enormouse wave twice her size.

sploooosh!

Nibbler jumped in with abandon.

SPLATA-SPLATA-SPLASH-SPLASH!

I forced myself to flop into the water.

At the same time, I tried to:

1. hold my snout

2. not lose my cloak

3. fill my cheeks with air (better safe than sorry!)

But as soon as I was **underwater**, I realized I could breathe just fine!

The seabed was quite a sight: There were houses made of sparkling mother-of-pearl surrounded by anemones that waved softly in the current. It was

AN UNDERWATER CITY!

An enormouse **shell** stood in the heart of the city. It looked like it belonged to a gigantic hermit crab! But going in and out of it were tons of dragons. Actually, they were a cross between

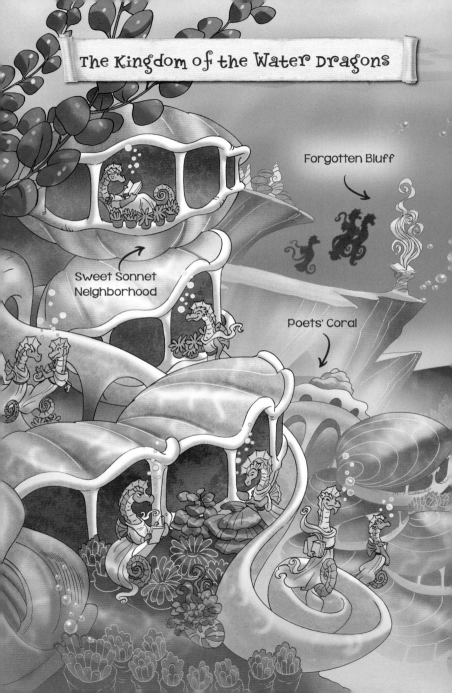

The Kingdom of the Water Dragons

Forgotten Bluff

Sweet Sonnet
Neighborhood

Poets' Coral

Ancient Poem Algae

Anemone of Poetic
Inspiration

Deep Blue Grotto

Library

Resonant Algae
Woods

Thoughtful
Path

dragons and seahorses!

I pointed it out to Maple.

"They are very different from the Forest Dragons."

"They live underwater," Maple said. "That's why they look like sea creatures. They are called

AQUA DRAGONS."

The aqua dragons fluttered lightly along, **waving** their tails. They seemed totally wrapped up in whatever they were thinking.

When they noticed us, two of them came over. One asked in a *friendly* voice, "We just saw you swimming through! Welcome, strangers — who are you?"

I swam forward. "Hello! This is Maple, Nibbler, and Jazzy, and I am —"

The other dragon opened his eyes wide and exclaimed, "Your **armor** is so bright — you must be the fearless knight! *Poeticus Happyheart* is my name, and I'm so glad that you came! But, my dear, what brings you here?"

I explained, "The Prophecy of Dragonia says that I will find the **most sincere** dragon of all in your kingdom. That dragon will help me free five princesses from a terrible witch . . ."

BOILING BUBBLES

Poeticus became serious and said, "Oh, my, how sad — that really is too bad! But as I always say, it's a problem to solve right away. We shall go to Her Majesty — the one and only **Queen of the Sea**! Knight, I believe that you are the best . . . but you're more silly looking than I would've guessed!"

I turned **red** from embarrassment. Rat-munching rattlesnakes,

Why did these aqua dragons have to be so sincere?!

I muttered, "What do you mean? Is it my fur?"

Jazzy giggled and asked the aqua dragons, "Do you always speak in rhyme?"

Poeticus's friend answered, "Oh, yes — don't you see, for we just love poetry! It's like a guiding lighthouse for us. I'm Squidmire, at your service!"

Nibbler was delighted. "I also **love** poetry! My cousins would always make fun of me for it."

That dragon was just like me — I loved to spend

all day with my snout in a book!

The two aqua dragons led the way into the giant shell I'd seen before. Inside, the walls were totally covered in shelves, which held THOUSANDS and THOUSANDS of smaller shells. They came in all colors and shapes.

Poeticus took one and handed it to Nibbler. "For the one who loves poetry . . . here's a GIFT to you from me!"

Nibbler blushed. "Thank you, but I couldn't —"

Before he could finish, the aqua dragon opened the shell and . . .

IT WAS A BOOK!

The **shell** was the cover, and the pages were made of **algae**.

Squidmire explained, "It contains poems of great beauty!"

"Wow, thank you!" Nibbler exclaimed.

We swam up eight flights until we reached the throne room.

Two other aqua dragons announced us by playing coral trumpets. Poeticus and Squidmire went ahead to explain the reason for our visit to their leader.

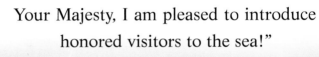
The queen was really very elegant. She had a coral crown on her head, a coral necklace around her neck, and coral bracelets on her arms, and she was seated on a magnificent coral throne!

Poeticus said, "QUEEN POSEIDONA, Your Majesty, I am pleased to introduce honored visitors to the sea!"

The queen called to her **handmaidens**. "Waverly, Rhyma, and Sandy! Please bring over the welcome tea!"

The aqua dragons brought over trays with four cups and a teapot made of decorated mother-of-pearl, and put them in front of Poseidona.

I grabbed a cup, but it **scalded** my paw! I immediately put it down, yelling, "Ouch! It's **HOTTER** than grilled cheese!"

Poseidona laughed so hard she made a wave of fiery **bubbles**, then said, "Careful, Knight! I'm glad it wasn't hotter — tea can still burn you underwater!"

What a CHEESEBRAIN I was sometimes!

After a few minutes, we all drank the welcome tea. It was greenish and tasted of algae, squid ink, and peppered mussels. Blech!

It was so gross that I made a face . . . and then I sneezed! *ACHOOOO!*

The force of the sneeze was so strong that I dropped my bottomless bag, which opened.

An avalanche of objects spilled out.

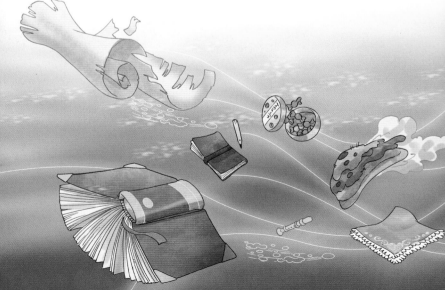

You see, before I left, I had taken advantage of the fact that the bag was BOTTOMLESS. Along with the gifts my friends gave me, I had added an embroidered lilac handkerchief from my dear aunt Sweetfur, a box of cheddar candies, and the notebook that I always kept in my pants pocket — now all floating around me! Lastly, Scribblehopper's BOOK fell out . . .

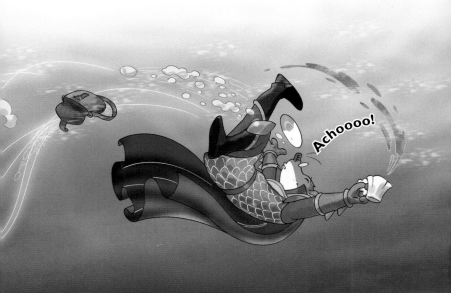

TRAVELS OF THE SOLITARY BARN OWL

The book had fallen open to a page with SCRIBBLEHOPPER'S "Ode to the Travels of the Barn Owl."

Curious, the Queen exclaimed, "These are verses, now I see, of a poet unknown to me. What luck! What a delight! A new poem is a lovely sight! Would you mind reading it aloud to this pleasant crowd? It would be pure joy, indeed, if we could hear you read."

After putting everything back in my bag, I said, "Your Majesty, it would be my pleasure to read it to you at your leisure!"

Oops! Oops! Oops! Oops! Oops! Oops! Oops!

I had started rhyming, too!

Oops! Oops! Oops!

But based on the expression on Poseidona's, Squidmire's, and Poeticus's faces, my rhyming was not up to their standards . . .

All the AQUA DRAGONS circled around me to hear the new poem.

"Th-the solitary barn owl w-was deeply sighing.
Alas! When I saw it, I felt like I was dying.
Poor feathered friend with his head hung low.
He'd lost his love — this sadness I know."

GULP!

The opening lines made my whiskers **droop** with discomfort! The aqua dragons didn't seem very enthusiastic about it, either, judging by the looks on their snouts.

Silence had fallen over the throne room. Not even the water was moving. One single boiling **bubble** rose up — who knows whether it was from a yawn or a toot! No one dared speak, but some dragons had covered their ears with **algae** . . .

I cleared my throat once

Poeticus

Sandy

Rhyma

more and continued reading:

"Your suffering, owl, as you
wander alone,
is a stab in my heart —
it makes me moan."

"Okay!
Knight, that's enough!

Someone had broken the silence with a cry: It was **Waverly**, one of Poseidona's handmaidens.

Desperately, she said, "Thank you for being willing to read, but I'm afraid this writing is not what we need! This tragic poem is such a bore — I would rather get seasick than hear any more!"

Jazzy, who had kept to herself up until then, exclaimed, "Oh, thank goodness someone said it! It felt like **so much time** had already passed that I was sure I'd grown a beard longer than my great-great-great-great-grandfather Tristan's."

Nibbler had actually fallen **fast asleep**.

At that point, my companions and I exchanged looks: Waverly was the only one who had the COURAGE to say that the poem was boring. She was the most sincere of all the Water Dragons!

WE HAD FOUND THE SECOND FROM THE ANCIENT PROPHECY OF DRAGONIA!

I said to her solemnly, "Waverly, you are the sincerest dragon in the kingdom! Would you join

Team Dragonia

and help us free the five princesses who are **IMPRISONED** by the witch Darkrock?"

Waverly responded, "I must be sincere: Darkrock fills me with **fear**! But with you, oh, Knight, I'll find the courage to fight."

"This is great news!" Jazzy said **joyfully**. "We need a frank and determined dragon like Waverly to **save** the princesses!" Then she gave Nibbler, who was still napping, a pat. "Hey, Nibbler, **WAKE UP**! Did you hear?"

But he kept on snoozing . . .

Queen Poseidona congratulated Waverly for her sincerity as well. She took off the coral pendant that she wore around her neck and gave it to Waverly.

"Here — please take my coral GEM. It will help you as you travel with them!"

Then all the aqua dragons blew millions of bubbles, which all formed a

Now that we had found the sincerest dragon, we were ready to continue on to the next kingdom: the Kingdom of the Mountain Dragons!

THE MOUNTAIN
DRAGONS

After saying good-bye to the aqua dragons, we flew toward the perpetually snow-covered part of Dragonia:

THE KINGDOM OF THE MOUNTAIN DRAGONS.

There, we would look for the wisest dragon on the island.

Frozen feta! It was so cold up there!

Luckily, the aqua dragon's breath warmed things up like a stove. Every time Waverly blew one of her bubbles, it let out **HEAT** that defrosted us nicely.

Despite the cold, the landscape was fantastic. Soon, we could see a pasture full of sheep with

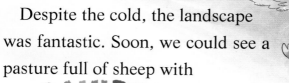

RAINBOW WOOL!

But they were all running to and fro . . . What was happening?

Maple said, "Those are **RAINBOW SHEEP**: They only live here in the Kingdom of the Mountain Dragons. But they seem scared, like something is bothering them!"

BAAAA BAAAA! BAAAA BAAAA!

We swooped down to take a look.

Nibbler exclaimed, "Oh no! Look, someone **BROKE** the fence! That's why they're free. And there are scraps of paper . . ."

Then Nibbler approached a large tree and added, "I recognize the MARKS on this bark! The **Scroungers** were here! They must have passed through to get their fill from the Mountain Dragons, and on their way, they left papers, SCRATCHED up tree trunks, and broke the sheep's fence. That's why the herd is so scared!"

Jazzy began to leap around in fury. "Get ready, you Scrounger **bullies**! I'll pinch your double chins!"

Maple said, "First, we need to think about the sheep."

We approached them very **slowly**, but the sheep were too scared. They kept running

HERE, THERE, AND EVERYWHERE!

"I have an idea!" Jazzy exclaimed. "Chuckles's **flute**! Let's try to play it to calm them."

What a great idea! I rummaged through the **BOTTOMLESS BAG** until I found the flute, then tried to play it . . .

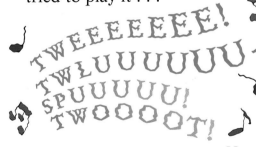

TWEEEEEEE!
TWLUUUUUU-
SPUUUUU!
TWOOOOT!

The flute was so **small** I could barely hold it in my paws, and I could only make some ugly, toneless sounds . . .

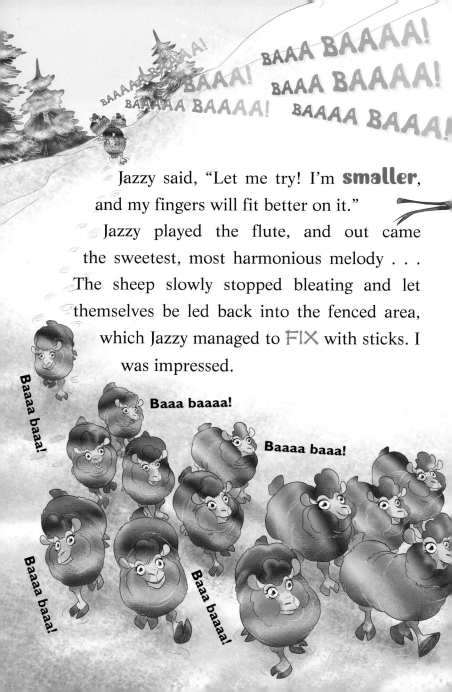

Jazzy said, "Let me try! I'm **smaller**, and my fingers will fit better on it."

Jazzy played the flute, and out came the sweetest, most harmonious melody . . . The sheep slowly stopped bleating and let themselves be led back into the fenced area, which Jazzy managed to FIX with sticks. I was impressed.

"How did you fix the fence without a **hⱥммɛr** and nails?" I asked.

She explained proudly, "You just need to wedge the wood in!"

Thanks to the skillful Jazzy, we had done it: The sheep were saved! But the **Scroungers** were still nearby . . .

Baaaa baaa!

Baaa baaaa!

WHERE ARE THE DRAGONS?

We finally managed to reach the **snowy peaks** where the Mountain Dragons lived. The mountaintops were so white that it felt like we were flying along a stretch of cream cheese. It was making me hungry!

They were so white that it seemed like no one had ever set paw on them.

So white that . . . wait a minute . . . maybe no one actually ever *had* been on them!

We landed on the side of a mountain, and I yelled into the wind, **"Is anyone there? Anyone?"**

anyone anyone anyone anyone? anyone anyone?

That echo was really strong! Was it even an echo?

I said, "Did you hear that? Maybe it was a **monster**!"

Waverly calmed me. "It's just the echo — have no fear. There isn't any monster here!"

I tried once more. "Hello? Anyone?"

anyone anyone anyone anyone anyone anyone anyone?

But only the echo responded. Then, once more, there was silence.

Squeak! It was quieter than a cat waiting to pounce. All that silence gave me more chills than the echo had!

I asked Waverly, "Are we sure this is the right place? There aren't any dragons here!"

Waverly said, "I'm sure it's here, Knight. There's no cause for fright!"

If dragons lived on those mountains . . . where were they **hiding**? Maybe they were ravenous Condor Dragons who lived perched on the tallest peaks, ready to swoop down and grab us with their claws. Or maybe they were

GHOST DRAGONS.
OR WILD YETI DRAGONS.

Waverly explained, "The dragons here are **shy** and on guard — life in these mountains is very hard. They're solitary and very **wise**. Let's be careful and seek with our eyes!"

Maple added, "They must be hiding from the **Scroungers**. Look down there!"

The sun was so **BRIGHT** on the snow that I had to squint. But soon I noticed that there were a few **CAVES** on the side of the mountain.

And there were **dragon prints** leading into them . . .

That's where the Mountain Dragons were hiding!

Maybe they had **heard** us arrive and feared that we were the Scroungers.

Cheese on a stick! We needed to find a way to communicate with them, but it certainly would be **RUDE** to go into their homes without an invitation.

Maybe a bit of kindness would work . . .

My friends and I landed in front of the caverns and approached the nearest one as quiet as a mouse.

It was darker than the inside of a cat's mouth.

HOLEY CHEESE! I WAS SOOOOO SCARED!

I was shaking from the tip of my whiskers to the tip of my tail.

"I-I'll **WAIT** for you here . . ." I said. "I'm too fond of my fur!"

THE KINGDOM OF THE MOUNTAIN DRAGONS

Scientist's Cavern

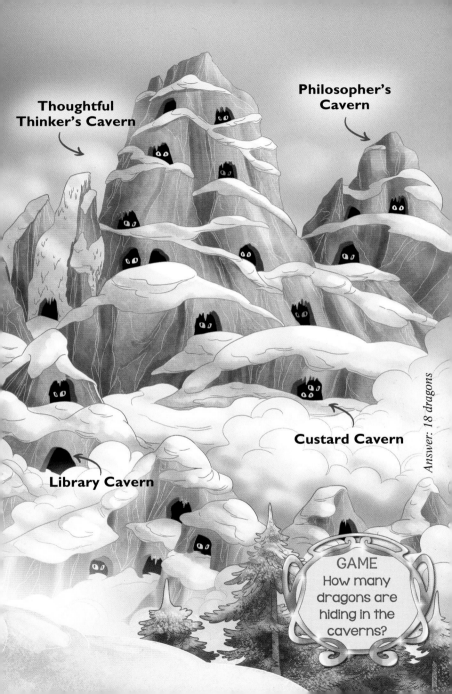

Thoughtful Thinker's Cavern

Philosopher's Cavern

Custard Cavern

Library Cavern

Answer: 18 dragons

GAME
How many dragons are hiding in the caverns?

Maple encouraged me. "Come on, Knight! You were the one who gave us our **COURAGE**! You have more than you think."

Jazzy continued, "**DARKNESS** is something that we gobble up for breakfast! We aren't afraid of anyone!"

Gulp! They were right. I could do this!

I stepped into the **CAVE** and muttered, "Excuse me, honored Mountain Dragons . . . May we enter? We are —"

ROODARRR ROODARRR ROODARRRR

Great Gorgonzola! An earsplitting roar ruffled my fur.

I jumped back, my whiskers shaking with fright.

The Mountain Dragons didn't seem friendly at all!

ROOOARRRR

Hang on, Jazzy!

Help!

Hang on, Nibbler!

A DRAGON
TOY

*R*otten ricotta! How would I ever find the wisest
dragon?

moldy mozzarella, why did
everything always happen to me?

I sat on a pile of snow and sighed. "First it was
the escaped sheep, now these bad-tempered
dragons. What's next?!"

I lifted my gaze and . . . Nibbler was flying near
the edge of a nearby CLiFF.

I called to him, "Nibbler, **be careful**! It's
dangerous!"

Jazzy leaped up and yelled, "What's happening?
Is there some Scrounger we need to nab?"

Nibbler responded, "No — there's something

I've got it!

here that must belong to a dragon cub!"

Maple, Waverly, and I went over. On the edge of the cliff, hanging from the end of the branch on a snow-covered shrub, there was a stuffed dragon toy!

Way down at the bottom of the cliff, there was a tumultuous river. If the toy FELL down there, no one would ever get it back!

Nibbler flew to the edge and reached out to grab the dragon toy.

Just as he cried out, "I've got it!" there was a gust of WIND — and the toy blew off the branch! But Nibbler grabbed it right before it fell.

Jazzy began to jump for joy. "Well done, Nibbler! Hooray for Nibbler!"

"That was so scary!" I cried.

Nibbler put the stuffed **TOY** on a rock. "There! This way its owner can come get it."

As soon as he left it, the snout of a **tiny little dragon** with pigtails poked out of a cavern. Then she ran over to the toy.

"Oh, little Star! Where had you gone?" she said to it, in tears.

She turned her shining eyes to Nibbler and said, "Thank you! You saved him!" And she gave Nibbler a big hug (even though she barely reached his knees!).

My heart MELTED like Brie in the sunshine, and I wiped my own tears away. I'm a very sensitive mouse, you know!

Two full-grown dragons came out of the cave and approached us. "We really don't know how to thank you! Our **Rubble** is very attached to her little Star."

Then, slowly but surely, one snout at a time, one claw after the next, all the other dragons came out of their caverns to come meet us. (Cheese niblets! The Mountain Dragons really were as **BIG AS MOUNTAINS**!) Thanks to Nibbler's actions, they knew that they could trust us!

A whiskered dragon with big sideburns said, "Our apologies for not being more **WELCOMING**. Usually, no one comes to these parts except those Scroungers."

Another added, "Plus, we're all a bit shy!"

"I am KING LICHEN," said the dragon with the sideburns. "And this is my wife, Queen Whitepeak."

"My name is Carabiner!" said another, with a beard down to his belly.

Suddenly, everyone was **COMPETING** to introduce themselves to us! These dragons didn't seem very shy at all!

Queen Whitepeak asked, "And who are you?"

I said, "We are Team Dragonia, and we are here to find the wisest dragon from your kingdom, who must help us rescue some princesses and defeat an evil witch."

King Lichen thought for a moment and decided, "We will talk it over around the **FIRE** tonight. We need to make up for the way we welcomed you. It wasn't very warm. I think we should start over. So we will light a bonfire and throw a PARTY IN YOUR HONOR!"

Jazzy exclaimed, "Hooray! I love bonfires! My family always organizes one to say good-bye to summer. Have I told you about my family yet? Well, there's my aunt Cheerful, who's the daughter of Grandpa Onetwothree and the sister of Uncle Happyjump, then . . ."

Before Jazzy could totally overwhelm them with her chatter, I cut in and said "Thanks, King Lichen! We would be happy to celebrate with you . . . and to warm up a bit."

There had been so much drama that I hadn't realized I was **freezing**!

THE WISEST DRAGON

S unset soon arrived and **COLORED** the mountains: The snow looked like peach ice cream. The Mountain Dragons were busy preparing the bonfire, and everyone was putting their **PAWS** to work. Some were digging a

hole for the wood, some were going to gather the wood, some were carrying large stones to

Hey!

make sure the **FIRE** was safe, and some were getting food ready.

Maple and Waverly helped carry heavier logs, while Jazzy and Nibbler were, er . . . losing a **snowball** fight to Rubble.

The little dragon was quite mischievous! She would melt Jazzy's snowballs with her breath before they could hit her, and she had great **AÏM**: In the twitch of a whisker,

my little pixie friend found herself under a pile of snow!

From beneath the heap she moaned, "Hey, that's not fair!"

Nibbler helped her out. "Come on, the king's going to light the bonfire soon!" he said.

It was evening by then, and everything was **ready**: There were blankets, and flaming pots with blueberry juice, and best of all . . .

There was lots of cheese! **DROOL!**

Smoked cheese for grilling, cheese kebabs, pots of cheese fondue, and bowls of ricotta to spread on bread. Yum! The one strange thing was that all the cheese was . . . rainbow-colored!

Queen Whitepeak explained. "I make it out of milk from the **rainbow sheep**. It's our specialty!"

My stomach was rumbling with hunger!

The queen's cheese was whisker-licking good. Not only was it **colorful**, but it was also full of many delicious and unique **flavors**!

Each mouthful had a different taste: blueberry, strawberry, walnuts, violets, spring water . . .

"It's delicious!" I said with my cheeks full of rainbow cheese.

Even Nibbler, who usually didn't eat too much, asked for Seconds of everything.

"Thank you, thank you!" he said. "Just a bit more, if it's no trouble. Thanks!"

Jazzy, on the other hand, was all wrapped up in a giant scarf and kept sneezing. "Achoo! Get out of here, you nasty cold . . . Achoo!"

Maple and Waverly were talking to the other dragons, exchanging stories about their kingdoms, while a dragon was playing the guitar in front of the raging fire.

It was a wonderful party!

The Mountain Dragons were very kind. But . . . how would we find the wisest one?

King Lichen began to speak. "It is a joy for us to celebrate the fearless knight and his valiant company. But a party isn't a party without **GIFTS**. Each of us would like to give you something you can take with you on your mission."

My fur turned **RED**. They'd already done so much for us! I didn't know how to thank them.

The dragons all lined up, each with a gift. Berryblue gave me a beautiful diamond and said, "It's the biggest and most precious one I have found in these mountains. I will give it to you so it can light up your way."

"Wow, thank you!" I said in disbelief.

Sunvalley brought me a **sled** with a lightning bolt painted on the seat. "This is faster than lightning! I will give it to you so you can flee from your enemies quickly."

"Thanks, Sunvalley!" I said.

Then it was Carabiner's turn. He gave me a

wooden sculpture and said, "I made it just for you!"

Another dragon gave me a scarf, another gave me a warm sweater, and another gave me a nice cup.

Finally, it was Peako's turn. He gestured, and everyone grew quiet. You couldn't hear even a single breath, just the crackle of the fire.

The mountains were wrapped in silence as we all looked at the dragon. What a magical moment! My whiskers trembled with feeling. What was Peako going to say?!

He took a deep breath, put a paw to his snout and said,

"SHHHHHH!"

All the dragons bowed their heads as a sign of understanding and respect: Peako's gift was the deep and marvelous silence of the mountains!

And in that infinite calm, we were joined by the same thought: Peako was the wisest dragon!

HE WAS THE THIRD DRAGON FROM THE ANCIENT PROPHECY OF DRAGONIA!

We were all tired from the exciting day, but we were also very happy about the new *friends* we'd made.

Before going to bed, I said, "Dear friends, thank you for the beautiful time we spent together! You have welcomed us with warmth, which we appreciate. And while we were sitting around the bonfire, we found the wisest dragon in the land. Peako, I hope you will do us the honor of joining us to help **free** the five princesses!"

The dragon looked at me with a SERIOUS — no, a **SUPER-SERIOUS** — no, the **MOST SERIOUS** expression ever.

Squeak! Did I say something wrong?

He bowed before me, then looked me right in the EYES . . . and exclaimed, "Yes!"

That NIGHT, we all had a long, relaxing, deep snooze, surrounded by the silence of the mountains. You couldn't even hear a fly buzzing . . .

Oops! Maybe I spoke too soon. It was Jazzy — she was snoring like a chain saw!

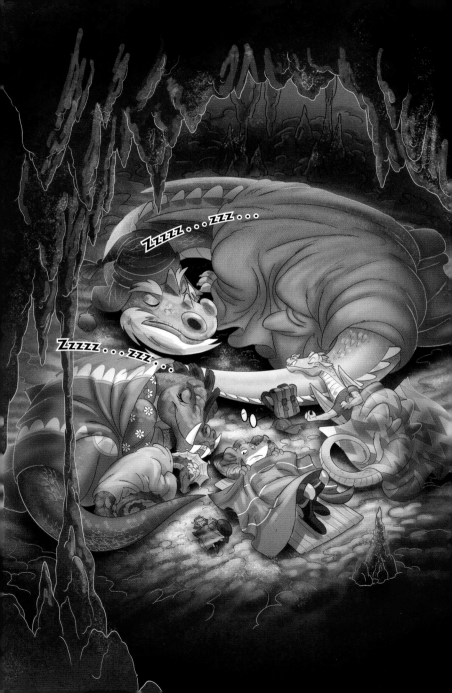

The next morning, after a breakfast of biscuits and **rainbow milk**, we thanked the Mountain Dragons once more and headed off again, now with Peako, the newest member of **TEAM DRAGONIA**.

We were ready to continue our adventure!

I squeaked,

"Off to the Kingdom of the Swamp Dragons!"

THE SWAMP DRAGONS

We left well-rested, **happy**, and full of energy. Now we just needed two more dragons to complete Team Dragonia!

We had been traveling for some time, when we flew over an enormouse *greenish* puddle full of weeds. Putrid Parmesan . . .

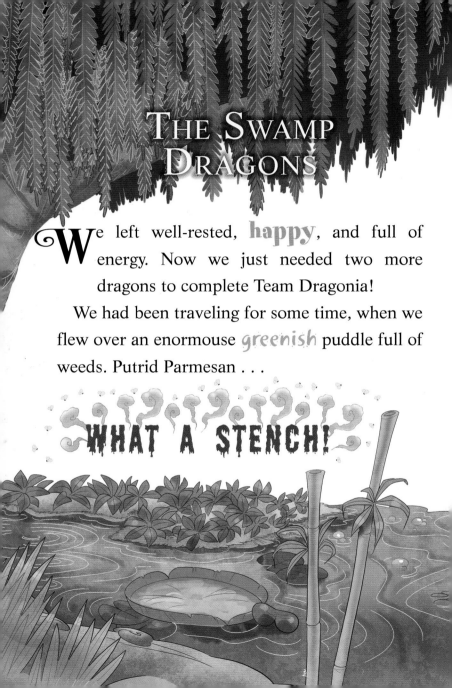

WHAT A STENCH!

Waverly exclaimed, "Gross! It's like rotten eggs and mold — if you jump in there, you won't live to be old!"

Maple announced, "We've reached

THE KINGDOM OF THE SWAMP DRAGONS!"

The swamp was full of large huts built on stilts sticking out of the **muddy** water.

"These must be the Swamp Dragons' houses!" I said.

We landed on the edge of a puddle and began to look around. Waverly barely managed to say, "It seems like there's no one —"

Just then, a giant **mosquito** sped by us with an extremely loud buzz.

"Watch oooooout!" he said as he passed.

The mosquito was wearing a shirt with the number 125 on it.

I said, "Did you see his shir —"

A swarm of a thousand mosquitoes flew past

us, making a deafening **BUZZ**!

They were all wearing shirts with numbers on them, like some sort of sports competition . . .

It was a `giant mosquito race`!

When the last of them disappeared, I was relieved. "Phew! That was rough!" I said.

"Really rough!" said a voice.

Who had said that?!

We turned around, and only then did we notice a strange FLAMINGO. He was flying upside down, with his head down just a few inches from the mud!

Jazzy took off her hat and bent upside down as well, then asked, "Why aren't you standing on one leg like all the other flamingos?"

He responded, "The world is more fun when it's opposite. Down becomes up, and if I'm sad, I get happy!"

DRAGON ART

Walking toward the stilt houses, we met a dragon who was scrubbing his back and singing, immersed in **GURGLING MUD**.

"Tralala tralala! What luxuring, what a delash, to be bathing in such trash! *Tralala tralala!*"

Waverly said, *"Luxuring? Delash?* Those aren't words! Is your head filled with cuckoo birds?"

The dragon stopped singing and turned red.

Tralala tralala!

"I play with my wordlings however I like! Who are you outsiders? What do you want from me?"

Waverly continued, "Of travel, we have covered a range — and your speech is really strange!"

I intervened. "Um, please excuse my friend Waverly. She is a bit BLUNT!"

But the dragon was furious. He came out of the WATER, yelling, "There's no respectitude for artists! I invent, I create! If you can't have beliefery, come with me and you will see."

Jazzy held back a laugh. "When did they practice *beliefery*? Back in the olden days?"

As the dragon put on his PAINT-SPLATTERED shirt, I translated. "I think he means to say, 'If you don't believe me, I will show you' . . ."

It didn't seem right to challenge him, so we followed him to a house on stilts. On the door was a lopsided SIGN:

GURGLE PRIDE
ARTISTIC
CREATIONS

"I'm **GURGLE**!" the dragon said as he opened the door.

Cheese on a stick! That place was incredible! The cabin was full — no, packed — no, bursting with stuff.

There were canvases; paintbrushes; jars; tubes of blue, red, green, orange, indigo, yellow, and violet **PAINT**; sculptures made of iron, clay, marble, wood, and granite; wrenches; chisels; hammers; pencils; erasers; markers; apple cores; potato chip crumbs; chipped mugs; books; drawing pads; tape; spiderwebs; and scrap paper. I had never seen a **mess** like this before!

Gurgle said, "To create, you need some confusitude! A REAL ARTIST must live upside down. Do you like my studio? Come in, come in!"

I took a careful step, saying, "May I —"

But as soon as I entered:

I put my foot in some **BROWN VARNISH** . . .

Then I tripped on a sculpture, which fell and got **SMUSHED IN** (the clay was still wet!) . . .

I grabbed a canvas for balance, **RIPPING** a huge hole in the middle . . .

Then I tumbled over two tubes of paint that opened suddenly, **SPRAYING** paint right onto the canvas that I had just ripped!

Moldy mozzarella, why did everything always happen to me?!

My friends had stayed in the doorway. They were staring at me, stunned.

I tried to apologize. "I'm sorry . . . I, er, didn't mean . . ."

But Gurgle lifted his PAW and stopped me. Without saying a word, the dragon stood the statue back up and looked at the ripped canvas and the splashes of paint. Holey cheese! He was going to be so mad!

That dragon would turn me into mouse meatballs and eat me for a snack! His silence was making my whiskers shake in fright!

I was ready for the worst, when Gurgle exclaimed:

"Fantastication!"

What? He *didn't* want to turn me into mouse meatballs? GREAT GOUDA, what a relief!

Gurgle studied the ripped canvas that was

covered in paint splotches. Ecstatic, he said, "What beautitude, what harmonity! Those works just needed a bit of wildation

I, er, didn't mean . . .

and a scratch of decisioness!"

At that moment, I remembered the

PROPHECY OF DRAGONIA:

After the courageous dragon and the sincere one and the wise one, it spoke of a dragon that was "silly — but also quite smart" . . .

Maybe I had just found him!

A GREAT PARTY AT THE SWAMP

Another dragon **burst** into the studio, alarmed by all the noise. She looked surprised and exclaimed, "It's **CHAOS** in here! Gurgle, you're so messy!"

The dragon exclaimed, "Mudelle! Let me introduce you to my outsider guests. My guests, this is

You're so messy!

Mudelle,

my heart!"

The dragon looked at me and said, "But . . . I know you! You're the **fearless knight**!"

Then she clarified, "Well . . .

fearless and maybe a bit **messy**!"

Mudelle was completely right: I was covered in **PAINT** from my snout to my tail!

I replied, "Yes, I'm Sir Geronimo of Stilton . . . and these are my friends Maple, Waverly, Peako, Nibbler, and Jazzy. We are on a **MISSION** to save five princesses from an evil witch."

Jazzy asked, "Are you all ARTISTS here?"

"Yes, of course! All of us!" Mudelle replied.

Now that we'd met another Swamp Dragon, I could see they were all a bit silly, so maybe finding the dragon from the prophecy wouldn't be easy . . .

Nibbler said, "That's zummmazing . . . smellazing . . ."

"Smellazing?!" Mudelle said, offended. "You mean to say that we **SMELL**?"

Jazzy jumped in and gave Nibbler her usual thump on the back.

"Amazing!" Nibbler said, "That's what I meant." He began cleaning up the room.

Mudelle relaxed. "Oh, okay!"

Then she added, "There's no need to put things in place, foreign dragon! Around here, guests don't have to do work. Come have some refreshments."

After cleaning myself up, we followed Mudelle, who introduced us to the other SWAMP DRAGONS.

Unlike all the other dragons we had met, the Swamp Dragons didn't have a king.

Gurgle explained, "We like to decisionate with suddentude. When we need to, we form a

M.E.S.S.
A MEETING ENTITY THAT'S STUBBORNLY SCATTERBRAINED."

And they'd decided to hold a banquet that night! The preparations took all afternoon. They

MENU
SWAMP DRAGON BANQUET
BY CHEF DRAGONFLY

SMALL PLATES:
GREEN ALGAE PASTA
WILD RICE CASSEROLE
CREATIVE SALAD WITH THIRTEEN GARDEN VEGETABLES

ENTREE:
RADISH HASH WITH FANTASY BREAD

OFF MENU:
CHEF'S SURPRISE
ANOTHER CHEF'S SURPRISE
YET ANOTHER CHEF'S SURPRISE (IF HE FEELS LIKE IT)

planned all sorts of PERFORMANCES, like juggling, miming, and theater. I was afraid all the food would be **mud**-based, but it turned out the Swamp Dragons loved good, healthy food.

Their chef, Dragonfly, served things like algae pasta, wild rice casserole, salad with just a little oil, and low-sugar pastries.

I was trying to bite into a roll stuffed with freshwater spinach when Peako got my attention.

Alarmed, he pointed above the reeds and exclaimed, "There!"

Rancid ricotta, it was the Scroungers!

How did they manage to find us? And were they really still mooching?!

Gurgle roared, "Those freeloaders!"

"We need to go find out what they're doing," Maple said.

So, as quiet as mice, we crept over to see what those **Scroungers** were getting into in the swamp.

There!

THE RETURN OF THE SCROUNGERS

We poked our snouts out of the reeds, careful not to be seen, and observed the Scroungers.

THEY WERE FIGHTING!

Mmmm . . .

Burp said to Burble, "Hey, I saw that — you took the last **apple core**!"

Burble answered innocently, "Me?! You're wrong, sister! I would never do that!"

The **twins** were about to really go at it, when Fillmeup, the tall Scrounger, said, "Mmmm . . . these **acorns** are so good! They're chewy and tasty!"

Meanwhile, Gargantus was

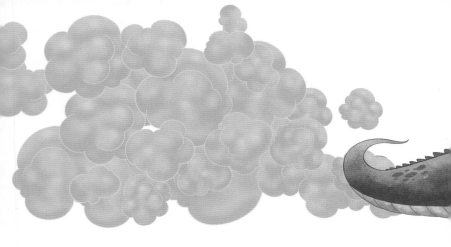

pacing in circles nervously, muttering, "Ugh! Look at what we're stuck **munching** on just to put something in our mouths. The Forest Dragons played a trick on us with that sack full of acorns! But we will get them! Our plan is perfect . . ."

poof

poof

Fullerton exclaimed, **"YES, YES, YOU'RE A GENIUS!"**

Gargantus ignored him and said, "We will **MOUSENAP** that Geronimo and scarf down the food from all the banquets thrown in his honor!"

CHEESE AND CRACKERS! Had I heard that right? Mousenap? **Me?!** How terrifying!

We needed to get our paws moving and **scurry** to warn the Swamp Dragons!

Come on, Scroungers!

We were nearly back when suddenly there was a *terrible smell*.

poof poof poof poof poof

Help!

Ugh! Scrounger gas! I looked up — the Scroungers were flying toward the banquet!

We reached the Swamp

Dragons, and I squeaked, "Heeeeelp! The Scroungers want to **MOUSENAP ME**!"

The Swamp Dragons quickly got up from the table. A dragon pulled out from the bushes a ⊏ATAPULT loaded with a **mud ball**.

The dragon unlatched the ⊏ATAPULT and launched the mud right at the Scroungers. "Take this!"

Stinkalicious mud ball incoming!

But the Scroungers managed to dodge it.

Dragonfly yelled, "Load up another

STINKALICIOUS MUD BALL!"

This time, the mud hit Gartantus and Fillmeup! Burp swerved to avoid it, and ran into Burble, who lost balance and BUMPED into Fullerton, who smacked into Fillmeup. What a TANGLE of wings, paws, and tails!

Gargantus yelled, "Retreat!"

In a flash, the Scroungers turned around and flew off. Hooray!

I was so thankful that my new *friends* had defended me.

Gurgle explained, "We are always prepared for the Scroungers' gorging! When we organize a banquet, we always keep the **ballshoot** ready. This time we got them dead on!"

"But they will **come back**, like they always do," Mudelle said. "And they will get the knight!"

Without realizing it, I had found myself in a

The Swamp Dragons (and the other dragons)

MEETING ENTITY THAT'S STUBBORNLY SCATTERBRAINED.

were all talking together, proposing a thousand solutions.

"Let's prepare a *disgusting* banquet!" Chef

Dragonfly suggested.

"We can build a bigger catapult!" Maple said.

"I have an idea!" said Mudelle. "Listen to this!"

When she finished elaborating, Peako began to walk in circles with his head down, thinking.

Gurgle muttered to me, "He must be the most sage-headed of all — we'll give him an ear!"

I approve!

He was right — Peako was the wisest, and we should listen to him!

Suddenly, Peako stopped and said, "I approve!"

Hooray! It was time to implement Mudelle's plan.

THE SMARTEST DRAGON

The following day, we waited until evening to prepare a **delicious banquet** that the Scroungers wouldn't be able to resist. There was even a dance performance. Everything was perfect.

FLAP FLAP FLAP FLAP FLAP
FLAP FLAP FLAP FLAP

GRUNT GRUNT GRUNT GRUNT
GRUNT GRUNT GRUNT

That was the unmistakable sound of the Scroungers!

They certainly didn't **waste** any time.

Gargantus yelled, "I smell something delicious! There must be food here!"

"Let's gobble it all!" Fullerton said, **drooling**. "Then we can deal with the mouse . . ."

Fillmeup pointed a **CLAW** at me and said, "Look! There's the knight!"

Burp and Burble screeched, "Let's grab him!"

The Scroungers darted downward and Gargantus **GRABBED ME** with his claws!

But he immediately huffed, "You're so heavy, you dirty rat. Is it the armor? Quick, help me carry him!"

The other **Scroungers** ran to help their leader, but as they got closer, the mouse in the dragon's claws seemed to shatter and got them all muddy!

Gargantus hasn't grabbed me at all. It was a sculpture that Mudelle had made! It was identical

to me, but full of the smelliest, most **rotten**
mud in the Kingdom of the Swamp Dragons.

Fillmeup yelled, "How stinky!"

Burp and Burble complained, "Yuuuuck!"

Fullerton exclaimed, "Gross! It's rotten!"

And they all disappeared into the night sky,
banging against one another on their way.

"Hooray! Mudelle's plan worked!" I exclaimed.

Gurgle said, "Those Scroungers won't show
themselves for a good while!"

I was so happy. Not only had we freed the
SWAMP DRAGONS from the Scroungers' raids, but
we had also found the fourth dragon from the
ancient prophecy!

I bowed deeply to Mudelle and said, "You are
the smartest dragon on the island. Will you come
with us on our journey? There is no doubt:

How stinky!

The dragon looked at me, stunned. "Oh, Knight! Thank you. It would be the grandiosest honor!"

Now we could leave for the last region of Dragonia: the Kingdom of the Field Dragons!

The next morning, at the first light of **dawn**, we took off . . .

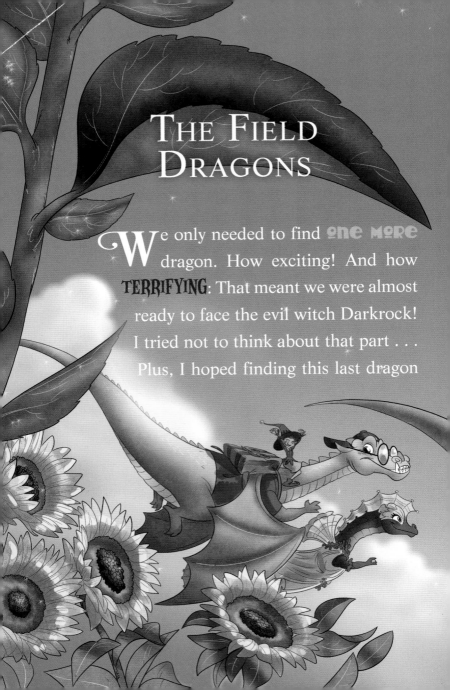

THE FIELD DRAGONS

We only needed to find **ONE MORE** dragon. How exciting! And how **TERRIFYING**. That meant we were almost ready to face the evil witch Darkrock! I tried not to think about that part . . . Plus, I hoped finding this last dragon would be fun — the **PROPHECY** said that we had to find the dragon with the greatest wit. So at least we might have a good laugh!

We arrived at the Kingdom of the Field Dragons after the sun had already set. Seen from above, the kingdom looked like an enormouse checkered blanket. It was divided into little **GREEN**, golden, **RED**, and brown squares. Soon we landed in front of a barn that was playing some *lively* music.

Jazzy jumped off Nibbler's back and began to

Waltzing Windmill

Dragon Hayloft

KINGDOM OF THE FIELD DRAGONS

The Solitary Tree

**Ancient Dancing
Dragon Barn**

dance. "The happiest dragon must surely be here! Listen to how **cheerful** this music is."

We pushed open the door, and . . .

"YAAAAHOOOOOOO!"

A pair of dragons bowled me over as they twirled to the music. I was **spinning** like a top!

I had ended up in the middle of a

dragon dance competition!

A band was playing onstage: There was a

Poor me!

dragon strumming a BANJO, one playing the HARMONICA, and another one singing at the top of her lungs.

Mudelle said, "Knight, I have an idea! Plunk over to me!"

I knew she meant to come closer to her.

She squeezed me into a dragon hug,

lifting me off the ground and dragging me into a wild tango as she yelled, "**OLÉ!**"

I have two left paws, but Mudelle was so graceful that both of us seemed like **expert dancers**! Everyone gazed at us in admiration, muttering, "**OOOOOOOH!**"

THE LOST PORTRAIT

The band onstage stopped playing, and the singer announced, "I believe we have found the WINNER of our dance competition! The dragon and the mouse!"

The dragons began to applaud enthusiastically. Me . . . the winner of a dance competition?! Great balls of mozzarella!

I said, "Thank you, but I'm no dancer! I'm Sir Geronimo of Stilton, and this is Team Dragonia! We are on our way to free five princesses from an evil witch."

The dragon who was playing the harmonica got off the stage and **stared** at me with piercing eyes.

Then, with his raspy voice, he said, "Mmm . . .

I knew at once that you were **no dancer**!"

I stammered, "W-well, I, er . . ."

Cheese niblets! That dragon was awfully big . . . What if he wanted to make mouse meatballs out of me?!

The dragon singer came off the stage as well and interjected, "Oh, don't worry about Harmon, Knight! He can be a GROUCH, but deep down he's sweet. My name is Dolly, and I am queen here. Welcome!"

Harmon leaned against the wall without

taking his eyes off me for an instant and said, "I've got my eye on you!"

If all the Field Dragons were like him, I would **NEVER** find the fifth member of the team! He didn't make me want to laugh — he made me want to cry . . .

WAAAAAAAH! **SNIFF!** **WAAAAAAAH!**

Wait a second — someone was already crying!

"I lost my family portrait! Waaaaahhh!"

It was Jazzy!

My poor little friend. I had never seen her so sad! She was sitting on Nibbler's paw and weeping.

I approached and gave her my aunt Sweetfur's lilac handkerchief. "Calm down, Jazzy," I said.

Jazzy took it and **sobbed**. "I've had it since was born! Now I can't look at it anymore when I'm feeling sad. Sigh! What will I do?!"

I tried to comfort her. "Let's **LOOK** for it. It must be around somewhere . . ."

Maple asked, "When was the last time you saw it? Do you remember where you put it then?"

Waverly tried to lift her spirits. "It'll be okay, Jazzy! We don't know where the portrait went to hide, but its memory lives on in you — deep inside!"

Waaaah! My portrait!

But Jazzy just sat on the floor of the barn, grief-stricken, holding on to the empty cylinder as **TEARS** ran down her face.

I had to do something for Jazzy. I couldn't continue my **MISSION** without helping my troubled friend first!

Dolly said, "Oh, have courage, little one! We are in the Kingdom of the Field Dragons . . . The only reason to cry here is because you're laughing too hard!"

All the dragons began to laugh and praise her.

"That's a good one!"

"Dolly, you're the best!"

"**HOORAY** for the queen!"

Then Dolly continued, "Listen here, Jazzy."

The pixie stopped crying for a moment.

Dolly said, "How did the **FROG** feel when he broke his leg?"

Jazzy shrugged, and Dolly shouted, "**UNHOPPY!**"

The Field Dragons all began to laugh once more.

The rest of Team Dragonia and I looked at Jazzy. She was the only one **not laughing**!

For the first time since I had met her, she was totally, completely, hopelessly SAD! Poor Jazzy. She had lost her smile.

Another dragon tried another joke. "What is the balloon's least favorite type of music?"

"*Sniff!* I don't know," said Jazzy.

"POP MUSIC!"

The pixie lifted up one corner of her mouth . . .

Cheese and crackers, maybe that had done it!

But a moment later, she went back to being SAD — VERY, VERY SAD.

I was starting to lose hope, when Harmon stepped forward. But he was so **grumpy**. How could he help her smile?

Harmon asked her, "What did the left eye say to the right eye?"

Jazzy shrugged without saying a word.

"Between us, something smells!"

The pixie stayed silent for a moment, then looked at Harmon and burst out laughing!

"HA, HA, HA, HA, HA, HA!"

"Thanks, Harmon!" I exclaimed. "You brought Jazzy's smile back!"

The dragon approached me, putting his paw around my neck. (Youch! He had a strong grip!) He said, "Hey, friend! At first, I really didn't like your **mousey** face at all. But I saw how much you cared about your friend, and for me, nothing is more important. You're one of us!"

I said, "Er, thanks! And you're one of us, too, Harmon! You're the wittiest dragon on the island, so . . .

YOU'RE THE FIFTH DRAGON FROM THE ANCIENT PROPHECY OF DRAGONIA!"

TEAM DRAGONIA!

Maple the Forest Dragon, **Waverly** the Water Dragon, **Peako** the Mountain Dragon, **Mudelle** the Swamp Dragon, and **Harmon** the Field Dragon, plus me and Jazzy.

Team Dragonia was complete!

It had been a long trip, full of adventure, many emotions, new friends, and **magnificent** new lands. But it was time to say good-bye to Dragonia. An even riskier adventure was ahead: a journey to the unwelcoming lands of **SORROWSTONE CASTLE**.

And I, Sir Geronimo of Stilton, had to **PROTECT** my friends, even if it meant missing them. I put my paw on Nibbler's back and said, "You have been a **fabumouse** travel companion, and I will never forget what you've done for us! But Darkrock is too dangerous — my whiskers are **trembling** just thinking about her! — and the ancient prophecy speaks of only

FIVE DRAGONS.

I think it's safer for you here in Dragonia."

Nibbler nodded and said, "I understand, and I will stay. I know you're doing this for my own good. It has been **fantastic** traveling with you all this far. I am lucky to have made friends like you. Thank you, thank you!"

Jazzy leaped to give him a big **hug** and was crying again. "Oh no, Nibbler! How will we manage without you?"

Maple hugged him, too, and said, "You have a courageous **HEART**. We are proud of you!"

Waverly murmured, "Nibbler, wherever we go, we'll think of you, you know!"

Mudelle, Harmon, and Peako joined the hug, too.

I added, "We're going to miss having you around. But we'll be back soon! At least, we hope so!"

RAT-MUNCHING RATTLESNAKES, I WAS TERRIFIED!

Peako sighed and shook his head sadly. We looked at him anxiously: His wise words would surely make this good-bye easier. He dried his tears, lifted his head, and said, "Good-bye!"

WHAT?! THAT WAS IT?!

"I'll wait for you here!" Nibbler said.

Dolly added, "You're always welcome here, and I'm sure you won't be bored!"

Once the last good-byes were said, we were ready to go. Without Nibbler there, Waverly had offered to carry *Jazzy*, and she climbed onto the dragon's back.

We took off, and I turned around one last time. Nibbler was waving his paw at us.

SIGH!

I would miss him so. But we needed to concentrate on our mission to Sorrowstone Castle: We had five Princesses to save!

The princesses are waiting!

THE TRIP TO SORROWSTONE CASTLE

Team Dragonia flew toward SORROWSTONE CASTLE. My dragon friends sped safely over the sea surrounding Dragonia, while I, the not-so-fearless knight, was not enjoying the height. I was such a scaredy-mouse!

Strange . . .

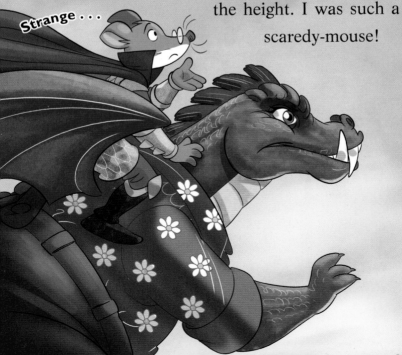

The dragons explained that to reach the Sorrowstone Castle, we had to fly north toward the **Land of the Pouring Rain**, the **HAIL HILLS**, and the **FURIOUS VOLCANOES**.

Holding tight to Maple's neck, I asked, "Are we s-sure there's n-no other way to get to Sorrowstone Castle?!"

Maple laughed and reassured me. "Stay calm! As long as we stick **TOGETHER**, we can face any obstacle."

I looked around. Enormous **clouds** were gathering on the horizon. They were **DARK**, full of rain, and seemed to be threatening us specifically!

"D-do you all f-feel like you're being w-watched?" I asked.

Harmon, who was flying next to Maple and me, responded, "Knight, I'll help you **relax**! What does ice cream do when it's upset?"

I stammered, "I d-don't know . . ."

Harmon replied, "It has a **MELTDOWN**!"

My friends burst out laughing. "Ha, ha, ha!"

Waverly said, "When you are very scared indeed, a *little joke* is all you need!"

Harmon managed to lift my spirits and help me forget my fears! (Well, almost . . .)

With Maple and her courage, Waverly and her sincerity, Peako and his wisdom, Mudelle and her intelligence, and Harmon and his wit . . . I was completely safe!

BOOOOOM!

Well . . . maybe just *somewhat* safe!

Scary **lightning** bolts darted through the sky. The clouds had filled the sky. A *VIOLENT WIND* overwhelmed us, tossing us up and down and back and forth.

Harmon yelled, "We are entering the

LAND OF THE POURING RAIN!"

No kidding. Thunder boomed all around us, and big drops of water began to fall on our heads! The dragons tried to fly faster, but the rain was so thick and so heavy that we were forced to slow down and fly lower.

Suddenly, Mudelle yelled, "Wait!"

I let go of Maple's neck and turned. **OH NOOO!** How was that possible?!

Waverly and Jazzy were imprisoned inside of a gigantic drop of rain! It was so **BIG AND HEAVY** that even though Waverly was an aqua dragon, she couldn't manage to flap her wings.

I squeaked, "They're falling!"

HILLS

We needed to **HELP** Waverly and Jazzy! Peako veered hard and flew toward them with all his might, then extended his **CLAW** toward the water bubble.

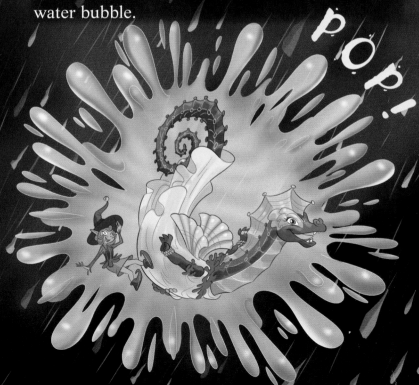

The raindrop burst, dissolving into a THOUSAND LITTLE DROPS. They were free!

"Thanks, Peako!" Waverly said, flapping her wings once more. "You may not talk very much, but your wisdom is extremely clutch!"

The dragon turned RED all the way to the tip of his tail and coughed, embarrassed . . .

We all held our breath: How would Peako respond?

Finally, Peako muttered two tiny words: "You're welcome!"

Meanwhile, the rain had let up a bit, but it had become really cold. Brrr!

With my teeth chattering, I said, "A-at least w-we're out of the Land of the P-Pouring Rain!"

TINK! TINK! TINK! TINK!

Harmon exclaimed, "Oh, for all the thorns on a cactus! What is that hitting me?"

TINK! TINK! TINK!

Frozen feta! The raindrops had turned to ice.

Harmon exclaimed, "Ah! We are over the Hail Hills!"

Those weren't hills — we were beginning

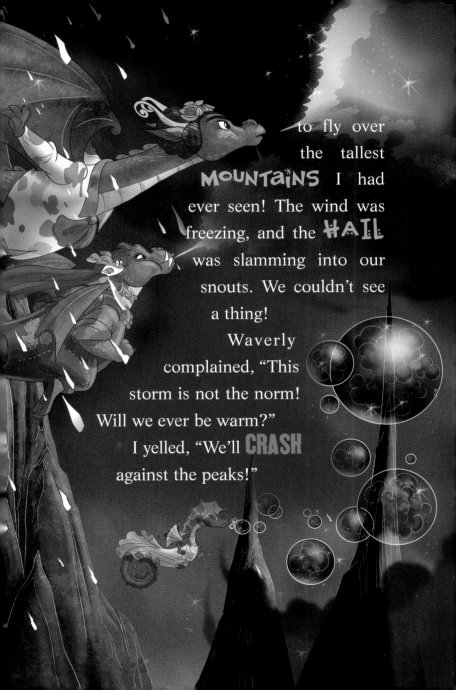

to fly over the tallest MOUNTAINS I had ever seen! The wind was freezing, and the HAIL was slamming into our snouts. We couldn't see a thing!

Waverly complained, "This storm is not the norm! Will we ever be warm?"

I yelled, "We'll CRASH against the peaks!"

This time, Mudelle came up with a solution. With a powerful flap of her wings, she flew above the rest of us and began to . . . breathe **FIRE** at the clouds.

"The hail is melting!" Jazzy rejoiced.

One by one, the other dragons began to breathe **FIRE**, too.

It was so hot!

So sweaty!
SO SCARY!
I closed my eyes and grabbed on tight
to Maple. I didn't want to end up
roasted like a marshmallow!
It got **HOTTER AND**
HOTTER AND HOTTER.
When would we pass over
these Hail Hills?
I opened my eyes and . . .

We were flying over a stretch full of enormouse **VOLCANOES**!

The lava was boiling like it was inside giant cauldrons. Bits of it were **shooting** upward, landing on Maple's paws.

I yelled, "What happened to the hail?"

Maple explained, "We have flown past the hills, Knight! This place is the Land of the *FURIOUS VOLCANOES*."

Holey cheese! First rain, then hail, and now lava?!

Mudelle yelled, "**LET'S GET OUT OF HERE, QUICK!**"

The dragons began to slip between the bits of lava. It was so scary!

I sobbed to myself silently, my tears evaporating immediately.

Just a few wing flaps later, we left the Furious Volcanoes behind us.

We stuck close together as we approached SORROWSTONE CASTLE. It was a dark silhouette before us.

Just a minute . . .

What was that on the horizon?

I asked my friends, "Did you see that? There's someone —"

"Stay calm, Knight!" Harmon said. "We are the only ones here. No one would dare come to these scary, **DANGEROUS** lands inhabited by the **wickedest witch** there ever was . . ."

I went paler than provolone. I really hoped he was right . . .

IN SORROWSTONE CASTLE

We had reached Darkrock's realm, and it was a chilling landscape. Everything — I mean **everything** — was made of STONE: the woods, the ground, rivers, and lakes. Even the clouds were stone! It felt very heavy.

In the heart of the stone woods stood a dark stone CASTLE that made my whiskers quiver. It was very tall and looked very, very menacing.

Peako pointed to it and said, "There!"

Yes, that was it, my dear mouse friends! That was

DARKROCK'S HOME!

Jazzy exclaimed, "Everything is so gray here! The princesses must be so sad."

Maple said, "We need to find them, fast."

Right at that moment we heard a cry. "**HELP!**"

From the tallest tower of the castle, five young maidens were waving their arms to get our attention. They were the . . .

PRINCESSES OF LOTUS FLOWERS,

the girls from the prophecy!

I gathered my courage and yelled, "Team Dragonia, let's go free them!"

The dragons sped up and darted straight toward

the castle. We could already **SEE** the walls below us when . . .

Oops!

My bottomless bag got caught on something. **Strange!** What could it have caught on in the air? But it fell

DOWN, DOWN, DOWN,

and disappeared into the woods.

Help!

I exclaimed, "My bag fell! I need to go get it!"

I couldn't lose the **GIFTS** that my friends had given me, and I couldn't go back to the Queen of Lotus Flowers without the prophecy **scroll**.

Team Dragonia darted downward. As soon as we reached the ground, Jazzy and I **JUMPED** off the dragons.

I said, "Friends, you head to the princesses. We will catch up with you as soon as we find the bag!"

The dragons flew away toward the castle. I could hear the princesses continuing to cry out, "**HELP! HELP! HELP!**"

Poor princesses! We needed to be quick and run to help the **dragons**.

We went into the thick of the **stone trees**. After a bit of walking, Jazzy called out, "There it is, Knight! Under that tree!"

Great Gouda, Jazzy was right!

We ran to get the bottomless bag, but as soon as I reached out . . .

A stone CAGE fell from the branches of the tree!

THUD!

Here's the bag!

In a Trap!

We were in a **TRAP**! Putrid Parmesan, how could this have happened?!

A thousand questions buzzed through my head . . . **Who** could have done something like this? Was someone **secretly** following us? Who set this trap? How did they know we were coming? How would we get free? But most of all: How would we free the five princesses now?

Moldy mozzarella, why did everything always happen to me?!

Looking around, I asked Jazzy, "Do you feel like we're being **WATCHED**?"

The small but determined pixie pulled the slingshot from her hat and pointed it toward the branches. "Come out and face us if you're

brave enough, marble face! Come out of your hiding spot, scaredy-stone! Come face Jazzy, you little . . . you little . . ."

"You little lump of Limburger," I suggested.

"You little lump of Limburger!" Jazzy continued, jᵘmpiⁿg like a spriⁿg.

Why does everything always happen to me?

Come out, marble face!

As she leaped to and fro, the pixie ended up out of the cage!

"You're free!" I exclaimed.

She was so **small** that, without even realizing it, she had slipped through the bars.

Jazzy jumped back over to me and said, "Now I will help you get free!"

Huff! Pant! We tried everything, but:

🐉 I was **TOO BIG** to slip through the bars,

🐉 the cage was **TOO HEAVY** to be lifted,

🐉 the ground was **too hard** to dig into,

🐉 and the bars were **TOO THICK** to be broken!

"We'll never get me out," I whined. "Leave me here, Jazzy. You go **help** our friends."

The pixie scratched her hat, thoughtful, then suddenly exclaimed, "Why don't you go into the bottomless bag?"

I looked at her, stunned. "What?! Me? In there? But it's tiny!"

Jazzy continued, sure of herself, "Anything can go in the bag — even **GIGANTIC** things. We already put a ton in there — a giant cookie, a poetry book, a flute, and all the gifts from the Mountain Dragons! I don't see why you can't fit in there, too. Then I'll pass the bag through the bars, and voilà, you'll be free!"

STINKY CHEESE ON A STICK!

Why didn't I think of that?

I put the bag on the ground, opened it, and looked inside. I thought, *What if I never manage to get out?* **Squeak! How scary!**

Jazzy encouraged me. "What are you waiting for, Knight? Come on!"

I responded, "Umm . . . It's **DARK** in there! How will I see where to put my paws? And what if the scroll rips? And what if —"

"Don't be afraid. I promise I will get you out," Jazzy said. **GULP!**

Jazzy was right. I had to do it.

① I put one foot in the sack, then the other . . . and finally . . .

② I disappeared inside. How frightening! I couldn't see my paw in front of me!

③ I felt Jazzy grab the bag and drag it out of the cage . . .

A moment later, the pixie yelled, "You can come out, Knight!"

④ I reached my paws out toward the opening of the bag, and felt around for Jazzy's hand. In a flash, I jumped out.

"It worked!" I squeaked. "Thanks, Jazzy!"

I grabbed the bag and felt reassured. I was so thankful for all of my *friends* and for all the help they had always given me during hard times, of the gifts they had given me, including the kiss that Blossom had given me. I held on to all the

love they had for me . . .

I could not let them down!

With newfound courage, I said to Jazzy, "Quick, **let's go**! We must run to the castle! There are five princesses to save!"

DARKROCK'S POTION

We reached the door to Darkrock's castle and heard a cackle of **laughter** above us. There never was a sound so terrifying!

We looked up and saw who was laughing. Above us, riding a broom, was . . .

A WITCH!

Holey cheese, she was petrifying! She had **grayish** skin, and she was holding a big glass vial in her hands.

Luckily, she hadn't seen us . . . or at least I hoped she hadn't.

Jazzy whispered, "That's Darkrock!"

Squeak! Just looking at her made my whiskers **tremble**!

The witch looked down into the courtyard of the castle and yelled, "You fell for it, dragons! You fell right in my **TRAP** like flies to honey!"

What?! What trap was she talking about?! *Carefully*, so we wouldn't be noticed, Jazzy and I went through the door and entered the castle's courtyard.

There, we saw our dragon friends — who had all been turned to

STONE!

They were five statues!

Before I could to stop her, Jazzy yelled, "Hey, you! Granite head!

Jazzy, careful!

Free my friends!

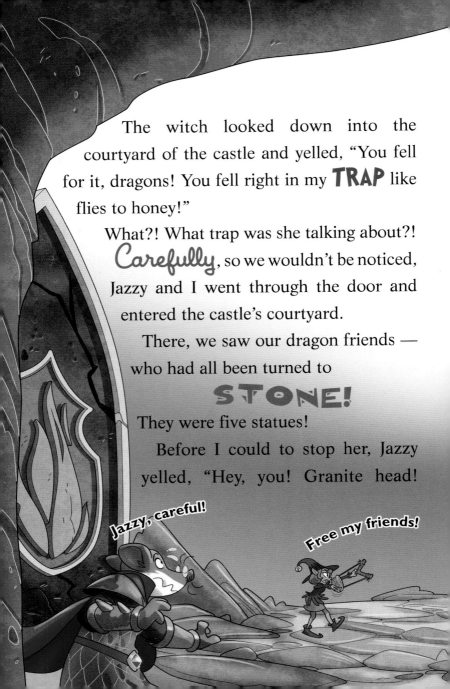

Free my friends

at once!"

I was terrified . . .

Darkrock would **CRUSH** us!

The witch turned suddenly. "What are you two doing here?!" she yelled. "How did you manage to get out of the **CAGE**?"

What are you doing here?!

Wait, what?! She was the one who had **imprisoned** us?

Jazzy exclaimed, "What do you care, you evil —"

I interrupted bravely, "Umm . . . it's a long story! But now, we will **FREE** our dragon friends, and the princesses, too . . ."

Darkrock snickered. "Of course, the princesses! You are all so predictable, you good guys! It's almost not even fun tricking you. All it takes is a few princesses in danger, a prophecy, and some good feelings — and game over!"

Jazzy jumped up. "Trick us? What do you mean, you nasty witch?"

She said, "I know the Prophecy of Dragonia. I kidnapped the five princesses on purpose so you would come save them with the **five greatest dragons**. I wanted to get them all together — so I can **STEAL** their precious traits. Yes, I know. I'm a genius!"

Rancid ricotta! She had the **WICKEDEST** laugh I had ever heard! And what a terrible trick.

Then Darkrock yelled, "GARGO! Come here at once, you incapable oaf!"

With a POOF and a cloud of gray smoke, a little stone gargoyle appeared next to the witch.

I recognized him at once. *"IT WAS YOU!*

GARGO

Gargo is a gargoyle and Darkrock's assistant. He takes care of all the tiresome work, from capturing the witch's enemies to preparing stone pasta. At night, when he's sleeping, he dreams of having giant wings, but whenever he gets to the best part, he is always awakened by Darkrock's screams for breakfast.

DARKROCK

Darkrock the witch is the ruler of Sorrowstone Castle, a desolate realm that's completely petrified and lies at the edge of the Kingdom of Fantasy. Her heart is as hard as stone, and she is incapable of having good feelings. She is selfish and wicked, and wants to turn the entire Kingdom of Fantasy into a sad wasteland of rock.

You were watching us during the storm, and you're the one who trapped us in that cage . . ."

The creature grumbled, "And the bag . . . I made it fall. It was pebble's play!"

The witch thundered, "That's enough chitchat! Take these two to the Treacherous Tower. And make sure they stay there while we brew the Potion that will give me all the dragons' powers."

The gremlin grabbed us with his chunky claws, straightened his head with an arrogant air, and . . . unfurled his pair of tiny little wings. To lift in flight and carry us would not be an easy task!

Darkrock, meanwhile, got off her broom and was beginning to caress the glass vial. "Soon the five-power magic potion will be ready! Ha, ha, haaaaa!"

Gargo flew slowly, but we soon lifted off the ground.

I yelled, "Umm, excuse me, **Darkrock**? C-could you tell me, what exactly do you need the five dragons' powers for?"

The witch snickered and said, "What a silly question. I need them, of course . . .

TO TAKE OVER THE KINGDOM OF FANTASY!

AND TURN IT

INTO A

DESOLATE

WASTELAND

OF ROCK!"

THE TREACHEROUS TOWER

Gargo had trouble flying. With every bat of his wings, he **LOWERED** down so much he risked scraping my tail on the sharp points of Sorrowstone Castle. Suddenly, my **PAW** bashed against one.

Jazzy yelled, "Careful, you flying lump!"

From above, the witch's **CASTLE** was even scarier: Those sharp rocks were like **TEETH** waiting to bite!

There was a wall surrounding the castle, and it linked the **FOUR** towers at its corners.

Who knew which tower we would be locked into? **Squeak!**

Meanwhile, Gargo was complaining. "A creature as noble and proud as me, called 'scrap rock'! How **DARE** she?!"

Jazzy exclaimed, "If you're so **NOBLE AND PROUD**, why do you do everything the witch says?"

Gargo coughed. "Mind your own business, you tiny pixie! You just worry about your friend over there . . . He's looking a bit green. Doesn't he like the way I fly?

HA, HA, HA, HA!"

We reached a tower that was so tall, slender, and wobbly that one of Jazzy's sneezes could have toppled it over. Gargo announced, "Here we are! The *Treacherous Tower*: your new home!

HA, HA, HA, HA!"

He flew us in through a tiny window, put us down on the floor with a **THUD**, and quickly flew away. Jazzy and I looked around. We were in a gloomy room with walls that looked like they were about to collapse.

As soon as I stood up and approached the window, the whole tower moved with a chilling cracking sound. **Slimy Swiss cheese**, that was not good! What would become of us?

I called to Gargo, "Couldn't you throw us in a dark, dusty basement? I'm afraid of **HEIGHTS**!"

Flying in front of the window, GARGO smiled wickedly. "I suggest you stay as still as stones," he said. "The tower is treacherous, after all! HA, HA, HA, HA!"

Then he disappeared with a POOF, leaving a cloud of gray smoke behind him.

"What now?" I said. "What will happen to our

dragon friends and the poor princesses?"

She sighed. "I don't know! We are too high up here! Even I can't get down. As it stands right now, we're trapped . . ."

My whiskers **DROOPED** in despair.

The King and the Queen of Lotus Flowers had trusted me with this mission, and I hadn't managed to succeed. Now what would happen to the Kingdom of Fantasy? And to me?!

Just then I saw a SILHOUETTE on the horizon. It was small, awkward, and was wearing . . . a pair of glasses!

Jazzy and I cried out together, "Nibbler!"

Trying to move as little as possible so we wouldn't shake the tower, we began to call and signal for him. "Nibbler! *Psssst!* We're here!"

When he finally noticed us, he flew through the window.

"How great to see you again!" he said.

Jazzy jumped up and **HUGGED** him so hard that the tower swayed again.

Nibbler asked right away, "What did Darkrock do to the other dragons?! Knight, you need to free them!"

"I will explain everything," I said. "But first, tell us: What are you doing here?!"

Our friend was all *bruised* up: He had gone through the pouring rain, the hailstorm, and all that lava . . . all by himself. Cheese niblets!

HE WAS QUITE A BRAVE DRAGON!

Nibbler said, "After you left, I thought I would do something useful, so I began to look for Jazzy's family **portrait**. She was so sad that she lost it! So, here — I brought it back." He took the portrait out of his bag and gave it to Jazzy.

The pixie was so happy, she burst into tears.

"Thanks, Nibbler! You are a *true friend*!" Jazzy said.

The dragon muttered, "Er, well, there's just one little problem. I found it in a puddle of **mud** in the Kingdom of the Swamp Dragons. It must have slipped out of the cylinder when you took off your hat to talk to that strange flamingo. So the **COLOR** is a bit smudged. I'm sorry!"

Jazzy unrolled the portrait and we looked at it. It was, in fact, very muddy and **smudged**.

The pixie said, "I'm happy all the same!"

I looked more closely at the portrait. The image was half-gone, but . . . under the color you could **SEE** something else. I took it to examine more closely, and I found that the portrait was made on . . .

A FRAGMENT OF SCROLL!

THE MISSING FRAGMENT

eneath the artwork, nearly completely faded, were some **words**! I could just barely read them:

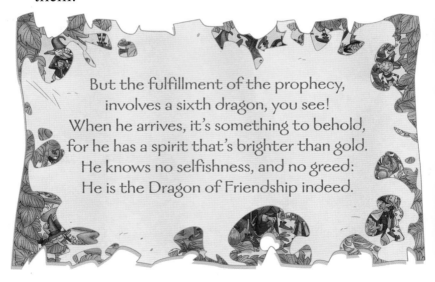

> But the fulfillment of the prophecy,
> involves a sixth dragon, you see!
> When he arrives, it's something to behold,
> for he has a spirit that's brighter than gold.
> He knows no selfishness, and no greed:
> He is the Dragon of Friendship indeed.

Nibbler and Jazzy listened with bated breath. Jazzy exclaimed, "How funny! Those **words** have always been beneath the painting and I never knew!"

"It seems like it's a piece of something else . . ." I said.

Of course!

Great Gorgonzola! Of course!

I took the scroll with the Prophecy of Dragonia from the bottomless bag. Then I put it next to Jazzy's.

THE TWO SCROLLS FIT PERFECTLY TOGETHER!

My friends and I stared in disbelief. For all those years, the last part of the Prophecy of Dragonia was **hidden** under that portrait!

I said, "The scroll must have **TORN** apart long, long ago . . ."

Nibbler added, "And the two parts got separated . . ."

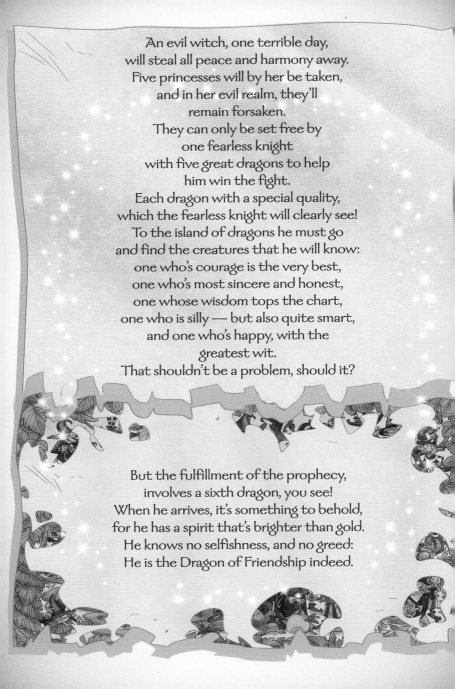

An evil witch, one terrible day,
will steal all peace and harmony away.
Five princesses will by her be taken,
and in her evil realm, they'll
remain forsaken.
They can only be set free by
one fearless knight
with five great dragons to help
him win the fight.
Each dragon with a special quality,
which the fearless knight will clearly see!
To the island of dragons he must go
and find the creatures that he will know:
one who's courage is the very best,
one who's most sincere and honest,
one whose wisdom tops the chart,
one who is silly — but also quite smart,
and one who's happy, with the
greatest wit.
That shouldn't be a problem, should it?

But the fulfillment of the prophecy,
involves a sixth dragon, you see!
When he arrives, it's something to behold,
for he has a spirit that's brighter than gold.
He knows no selfishness, and no greed:
He is the Dragon of Friendship indeed.

And Jazzy concluded, "And they ended up in two different places in the Kingdom of Fantasy!"

Everyone — Darkrock included! — had always believed that the **PROPHECY** foretold **Five** dragons, but really there were **Six**. Only now that we put the pieces together was the prophecy complete!

I said, "This last part of the prophecy talks about a *dragon with a spirit brighter than gold,* a dragon who isn't selfish or greedy . . ."

I realized that that dragon was right there under my snout!

"Nibbler!" I exclaimed.

"YOU MUST BE THE SIXTH DRAGON FROM THE PROPHECY!"

Nibbler looked at me, stunned. His cheeks turned all different **shades** of red.

His voice thick, he said, "I am truly lafftered . . . traflered . . ."

Jazzy gave him her usual THUMP on the back, and he continued, "Flattered! But . . . I can't be that dragon. I am not so imtorpant . . . timpornant . . . imp —"

Instead of thumping him on the back, Jazzy finished Nibbler's sentence for him. "Important! Important! Important!" And jumping around happily, she continued, "Of course you are **important**, my friend! So very, very important!"

I bowed before him to mark the *solemnity* of the moment, and announced, "Nibbler, in addition to being a loyal and kind friend to all of us, you faced many dangers just to give your friend back her smile. You are the only one who could be . . .

the dragon of friendship!

I am sure of it! And now you have an important task to carry out: to break the spell that is imprisoning the other dragons, and to free the princesses."

You are the dragon of the prophecy!

That's impossible . . .

Hooray!

Then I explained to Nibbler how Darkrock had led us to her kingdom by fooling us in order to steal our friends' qualities and transform them into a Potion that would make her extremely POWERFUL.

Once I finished the story, Nibbler exclaimed, "Quick! Grab on to me: I will get you out of here!"

Jazzy and I obeyed, and as we dashed out of the tower window, my whiskers shook with pride. Nibbler really was

a true, generous, unstoppable dragon of friendship!

As we flew, we were surrounded by a most delicate scent . . . It was the fRaGRaNce of fRieNDSHiP!

THE PETRIFYING SPELL!

We landed on the walls that linked two of the towers of SORROWSTONE CASTLE and looked down onto the courtyard. With powerful magic, Darkrock was sucking the energy from the dragons and transferring it to her vial!

RAT-MUNCHING RATTLESNAKES, THAT WASN'T GOOD!

My whiskers were shaking in fright. How could just the three of us defeat such a wicked and powerful witch?

At that moment, a voice behind us squawked, "Where do you think you're going?"

It was Gargo! He had discovered us!

Then he yelled, "YOUR ROCKY SHARPNESS, the prisoners are getting away!"

Darkrock saw us and jumped on her broom. "Excellent! It seems you can't wait to be **TURNED TO STONE** like your friends," she yelled. "Your wish is my command! Mouse, I'll turn you into a granite paperweight. The pixie will become a lava stone statue, and you . . . You! **Who is this dragon?!** How did you get here?"

Nibbler tried to talk. "I . . . I . . . I . . ."

But Darkrock didn't wait for him. "Well, what does it matter? I'll **PETRIFY** you as well, and then I'll finish the **spell**!"

But Nibbler was already petrified with fear!

I tried to encourage him. "Believe in yourself, my friend! Remember: **You are the sixth dragon of the legend!**"

The witch was amused. She said, "What?! Did I hear that right? He is supposed to be one of the dragons of the prophecy?"

She pointed a withered finger at me and said,

"There are only **Five** dragons in the prophecy. Everyone knows that, mouse. This thing is just a **potato** with wings!"

Gargo burst out laughing as he flew by upside down. "Ha, ha, ha! A potato with wings!"

Nibbler slumped over and didn't speak. On no! He had lost his COURAGE, like when he was with the Scroungers!

Jazzy yelled, "**GET LOST**, nasty witch! I will show you what happens to those who offend my friend!"

I said to Nibbler, "Don't believe **Darkrock**! She just wants you to lose faith in yourself."

The witch thundered, "That's enough! The time has come to PETRIFY YOU!"

"No!" Jazzy cried. "Nibbler, you can do it! You can free the dragons!"

He stammered, "I — I can't manage! I . . . I'll never be able to!"

I called out, "Only **you** can free the five dragons and complete the prophecy!

The power of friendship is inside you!"

Nibbler looked at us. He was gaining confidence, and was about to say something, but Darkrock didn't give him time. She extended her hands toward us and hissed, "You miserable creatures, prepare to taste the **POWER OF STONE**!"

Only you can free them!

You can do it!

THE DRAGON OF
FRIENDSHIP

I closed my eyes. If I had to become a paperweight, I at least did not want to see it happen.

But in a flash, Jazzy opened the bottomless bag and took out Mixy's **Shortbread Swirl** (which had become as hard as a rock!) and cried, "Have a taste of this cookie, you gravel-eater!"

She tossed it like a Frisbee, and the cookie hit Gargo straight on . . .

Take this, gravel-eater!

BONK!

He tumbled onto Darkrock . . .

BONK!

And she was thrown
from her broom just as she was
casting the **petrifying spell**, knocking
it astray.

The vial with the dragons' powers
slipped out of her hand and **BROKE** into
a thousand pieces, making the contents
evaporate.

"I'm sorry, Your Rockiness!" Gargo cried. "I
didn't mean to ruin your spell!"

Jazzy **cheered**. "Two bull's-eyes for one!"

I yelled, "Quick! Nibbler! Fly! **Believe in
yourself!**"

Nibbler gathered his courage and said, "Team Dragonia, I'm on my waaaaay!"

He darted toward the **STONE** dragons in the center of the courtyard and landed in the middle of them.

Then he looked up toward me and Jazzy and asked, "Now what do I do?"

From up on the wall, I yelled once more, **"Believe in yourself!"**

Nibbler stood still and then closed his eyes.

Jazzy looked at me, worried. She said, "Knight, nothing's happeni —"

But she didn't finish her sentence, because . . . a

began to surround Nibbler.

"It's the power of friendship!" I squeaked.

The light quickly grew until it became a giant sphere that surrounded all the dragons . . . and they came **alive** again!

"Hooray for Nibbler!" Jazzy cheered.

The Dragon of Friendship had **BROKEN** Darkrock's terrifying spell! The strongest power truly comes from unity and friendship.

Maple stretched her wings with a **creeeeak**!

Then she exclaimed, "My joints are still be a bit petrified!"

Harmon said, "Good morning! I slept like a **ROCK** . . ."

Waverly muttered, "Ouch, ouch, ouch!"

And Mudelle grumbled, "Oof, oof, oof!"

Peako bent backward, **cracking** the whole way, then he bent forward, stretched his wings, waved them a bit, and said, "Gee!"

When they saw Nibbler, they realized what had happened, and all cried out:

"Nibbler! You saved us!"

THE PETRIFIED WITCH

Darkrock, on the other hand, was more **furious** than ever. Riding on her broom, she flew in circles over the dragons, impatient to perform the biggest spell of her life.

Squeak! How scary!

Suddenly, her voice thundered, "What a moving scene! Well done — go ahead and hug! This way I only have to use one superpowerful . . . *PETRIFYING RAY*!"

Darkrock waved a hand in the air, creating an enormouse gray ray of magic that she directed straight at the dragons.

But Team Dragonia was ready. Quicker than you could twitch your tail, the dragons joined paws and united their energy, making a **magical shield** that repelled Darkrock's attack. The petrifying ray **BOUNCED** off — and went straight back to where it had come from.

"NOOOOOOOOOO!"

the witch screamed until she was turned to stone.

"NOOOOOOOOOO!"

echoed Gargo, trying to shield himself behind her. But it didn't work. He and his mistress had become two solid **STONE** statues!

Jazzy and I cheered from our viewpoint above. "Yippee! Hooray!"

Team Dragonia defeated the witch!

Then I yelled to the dragons, "Quick, let's free the princesses! Reflected spells only last a **short** while. Darkrock will wake up again soon!"

Waverly commented, "Oh my, that's too bad! If she stayed a 𝕤𝕥𝕒𝕥𝕦𝕖, no one would be sad!"

Nibbler said, "If you're right, Knight, I'd prefer not to be around for it!"

The **dragons** left Darkrock and Gargo in the courtyard and flew up to Jazzy and me on the wall. Maple said, "Jump on up, Knight!"

I positioned myself between her wings, and

We did it!

Jazzy got on Nibbler. Then together we all flew toward the **TALLEST TOWER**, where the princesses were.

"Heeeeelp! Heeeelp! We're up here!" they cried. I could tell they were worried.

Poor princesses!

Finally, their terrible adventure would soon be over!

PRINCESS RESCUE!

When we reached the top of the tallest tower, the princesses were waiting for us. The stone bars that had kept them imprisoned had **vanished** when the witch was **PETRIFIED**!

When I got off Maple's back, I shed a small tear of pride. After all the dangers and terror, we were going to bring the five princesses home and fulfill the true Prophecy of Dragonia!

I smiled and introduced myself. "Hello! I am Sir Geronimo of Stilton. The noble Team Dragonia and I are here to free you and take you home, to

THE KINGDOM OF THE LOTUS FLOWERS!"

The five princesses looked at us doubtfully.

Er . . . had my **speech** been that bad?

But then a moment later all five of them ran toward us, yelling, "Jazzy!"

The pixie leaped toward them, screeching, "Princesses!"

They all hugged tight, **happy** to be reunited. My whiskers were trembling with emotion, and I saw a large TEAR trickle down Nibbler's snout.

A princess with a **GREEN** dress came toward me. "Why did you **KIDNAP** Jazzy, Sir whatever-your-name-is?" she demanded. "I'm going to tie your whiskers to your tail . . ."

I was about to explain that I *hadn't* kidnapped Jazzy, but I didn't have time, because a princess dressed in **BLUE** said, "Leona, I must be honest. You are picking a fight, as usual!"

Waverly said, satisfied, "I can say

without fear — that princess is sincere!"

Then a third princess, dressed in WHITE, declared, "Vera, the wisest thing to do is to be quiet and listen to what he has to say."

Peako looked at the princess, surprised, and said, "I agree!"

Jazzy attempted to cut in. "Excuse me, princesses —"

"That's enough with the advice, Olivia!" interrupted a princess with a light PINK dress. "I, Sonia, will find out if they kidnapped her and if Mom and Dad knew what was happening. Tell us: Who are our parents and what are their names?"

Mudelle laughed and answered, "You show signs of smartitude! They are named Lotus and Lily, and they are the reigning crowns of the Lotus Flowers."

The fifth princess, who was dressed in YELLOW, said *"Smartitude?* I love it! That's funnier than one of my jokes, or my name isn't *Allegra*! Ha, ha, ha!"

Harmon said, "There's no denying it — I like this princess already!"

Cheese and crackers, the dragons and the princesses were getting along so well! Then I realized they had the same traits . . .

because their two kingdoms were deeply connected!

Before the conversation could continue, Jazzy intervened. "We came to **save** you."

"Sorry, well — I don't mean to rush . . ." Nibbler said at that point. "But **Darkrock** could wake up at any moment . . . so . . ."

Leona stepped in front of her sisters. "I'll **defend** you!"

Vera replied, "It's better if the dragons defend us . . ."

"And it would be wise to **leave** at once!" Olivia added.

Sonia took a pencil from her hair, fished a notebook from her pocket, and said, "According to my calculations, Darkrock should wake up —"

Allegra interrupted, "Speaking of calculations, why did the math book look so sad? Because it had so many problems! **Ha, ha, ha!**"

This was getting to be too much. "Double-twisted rat tails!" I exclaimed. "Let's get out of here once and for all!"

The five princesses and the five dragons looked at me silently for a moment.

Then they all cried:

"We're going home!"

THE KINGDOM OF LOTUS FLOWERS

hen we arrived back at the Kingdom of Lotus Flowers, I was totally wiped out. It had been quite a journey!

But we had completed our mission:

THE PROPHECY OF DRAGONIA WAS FULFILLED!

My whiskers trembled with excitement at the idea of seeing King Lotus, Queen Lily, and Blossom.

When they saw us approach, the king and queen were ecstatic. They *RAN* to their daughters and hugged them joyfully.

Blossom exclaimed, "Knight! You did

it! We knew we could count on you."

Thanks, Knight!

My heart swelled. "Um, well, it was thanks to the dragons most of all . . ."

Queen Lily hugged the princesses one by one and said, "What a **JOY** it is to see you again!"

Blossom got the chest with the crowns and exclaimed,

"Princesses, here are your crowns!"

The princesses happily put them on. Then the king and queen came over hugged me. "Thank you, Knight!" they said. "You have given us back our happiness!"

GAME
Harmon has
lost his hat ...
Can you find
it?

Answer: The hat is on Mixy's tray on the left side of the picture.

Then they went to shake the **PAWS** of each one of the dragons, saying, "It is an honor to meet you! And now let us all celebrate together!"

The celebratory **banquet** was magnificent. All my old friends from around the Kingdom of Fantasy were there, and Jazzy's family came!

When everyone had arrived, the king asked for silence and said, "Thanks to this courageous team of dragons, our five daughters are free, and the **KINGDOM OF FANTASY** is saved from the grasp of a wicked witch. That is why I have decided that you all deserve the

Valient Hero Medal!"

He called for Alyssum, the court page, to bring over the medals, and he placed them on the dragons' chests.

Cheese niblets, how **exciting**!

Queen Lily continued, "Nibbler, the knight told

me your whole story. We are all very appreciative. Would you like to stay here with us in the *Kingdom of Lotus Flowers*?"

Nibbler was clearly embarrassed, but replied, "Thank you, thank you! It would be such a great pleasure! I am truly nonored . . . ronhord . . . hornerd . . . **HONORED**!"

Jazzy said proudly, "Well done, Nibbler! You did it without my help!"

The queen smiled and said, "Dear pixie, you were also very valuable on this **MISSION**. And I have a special surprise for you . . ."

Jazzy's aunts, uncles, grandparents, and cousins gathered around, and her great-great-great-great-grandfather Tristan gave her a **rolled-up-scroll**. Jazzy opened it, and . . .

It was a new family portrait!

TEAM DRAGONIA

Moved, Jazzy whispered, "It's even more beautiful than the first one!"

At that point, Blossom said, "I thought that you would like to carry your friends from **TEAM DRAGONIA** with you as well."

A dragon came from the back of the room and gave Jazzy another, much smaller, scroll.

It was a portrait of Team Dragonia!

"Thanks! I will always keep it with me," Jazzy said, happier and happier.

The party was so fabumouse. I tried all kinds of delicacies — fruits, cheeses, cakes, smoothies, pastries . . . In the end, I collapsed on a sofa, closed my eyes and . . .

ZZZZ ZZZZ ZZZZ ZZZZ

I fell asleep thinking of the portrait of Team Dragonia.

BACK IN NEW MOUSE CITY

When I opened my eyes, a mouse dressed in **PURPLE** was pulling at my jacket. (Where was my armor?!)

"Gerrykins!" Creepella said. "Finally, you're awake! You were dancing with Tremblina, and suddenly . . . you fell and bumped your snout on the floor."

"Huh?" I said. "What? Sorry, princesses . . . at your service!"

Creepella stared at me threateningly and said, "Princesses?! What princesses are you talking about? Wasn't dancing with Tremblina enough for tonight?"

Tremblina? Who was that? And what was Creepella doing in the Kingdom of Lotus Flowers?

Oh, of course! Now I remembered!

I had been dancing with Tremblina and she was twirling me around like a top when I guess that I'd . . . **fainted**!

I jumped to my paws, looked around, and exclaimed, "I'm in New Mouse City! I'm home!"

I hugged Creepella and cried, "It's so good to see you!"

Compared to those bickering princesses, Creepella was as sweet as a cheesecake.

Creepella chirped, "It's so good that you woke up. We were starting to worry."

"Don't you worry about me," I said. "I just have a very big headache."

Trap arrived right at that moment and said, "My dear Creepella,

It's so good to see you!

can't you see that the thing Geronimo is best at is sleeping? I'm the *dancer* for you!"

He took her **PAW** and pulled her back out on the dance floor.

Tremblina said enthusiastically, "Let's get out there, too!"

She *DRAGGED* me out into the crowd once more. I tried to object, I really thought I should get some rest

But before I could squeak . . .

1 I **tripped** over my paws,
2 I **stumbled** forward,
3 I GRABBED on to her so I wouldn't end up snoutfirst on the ground.

PHEW! SAVED BY A WHISKER!

Then I would've thanked Tremblina for helping me, but before I could, I stumbled right onto her.

HOW MOUSETASTICALLY PAINFUL!

I scurried away. I was completely exhausted . . . and embarrassed!

It had gotten very late, and I couldn't wait to go home and curl up in bed.

Ouch!

When we reached the *grand hotel*, where Tremblina was staying, she hugged us all and said, "Thanks for the wonderful day! And come find me soon in Mysterious Valley!"

Umm . . . I think I'd need to recover from my mission to Sorrowstone Castle first!

Umm, I'll be busy for a while . . .

Of course!

A FABUMOUSE
SURPRISE

The next morning, I woke up to my phone ringing.

**RIIIING RIIIING
RIIIING RIIIING**

I got up at once — I had work to do at *The Rodent's Gazette.*

It was my sister, THEA, on the phone. "Gerry Berry! You're out of bed, right? I have a favor to ask you!"

A favor?! Didn't I JUST do her a big favor?

I said, "Er, okay . . . It's just that I need to go to the office today . . ."

Thea insisted, "I know, but it will just take a

second! Let's meet during your lunch break and I'll explain."

Oh no . . . Compared to this, the life of a fearless knight seemed like a vacation. I really missed my Fantasian friends! I went to the office, and while I was writing at least 375 emails, responding to at least 456 phone calls, and editing at least 97 articles, I kept thinking about them.

Maple, *Waverly*, Peako, *Mudelle*, Harmon, Jazzy . . . and Nibbler, the timid dragon who had discovered a great power within himself!

Who knew when I would see them again . . .

I was so wrapped up in thought that lunchtime came in the flick of a whisker.

Before I went out, I finished signing the last of the contracts and went over all my appointments for the week with Mousella.

Oh no! I remembered Thea was waiting for me. I was running late, as usual! I scurried to our meeting and . . .

Cheese sticks, what a fabumouse surprise! My sister came to meet me with

TWO CONES FROM MY FAVORITE ICE-CREAM SHOP!

Handing me the bigger one, she smiled and said, "This is to say thank-you for being Creepella and Tremblina's tour guide!"

It was the biggest, most delicious ice-cream cone I had ever seen. There was sweet ricotta, whipped cream cheese, creamy Colby jack, and even some candied cheddar, all covered with Parmesan . . .

slurp!

There's nothing nicer than taking a moment to stop and spend time with the people we **love**, don't you think?

How yummy! My heart swelled with happiness, and I said, "Thanks, Thea!"

Thanks, Thea!

When I went back to the office, I was so happy and relaxed that I decided the moment had come: I would start to write a B O O K about the newest adventure I'd had on the Island of Dragons.

I sat at my desk and wrote all day and all night, and all day and all night, and all day and all night . . .

Finally, when I couldn't keep my eyes open any longer, I typed the last pages of the story and fell

FIRST DAY

SECOND DAY

asleep!

But the book was finally finished! It told of the **PROPHECY OF DRAGONIA**, of how I had survived a mouserific adventure on the wings of powerful dragons in order to help the King and Queen of Lotus Flowers save their five princesses — and the entire Kingdom of Fantasy.

And it told of a witch who turned everything to **STONE**, and of a legendary team ready to face whatever came in the way of their mission . . .

THIRD DAY

ZZZZZZZZZZZZZZZZZZ

Well, yes, dear rodent readers! It's the book that you have in your paws right at this moment!

I hope that you liked it and that you will always carry Team Dragonia in your hearts, just like I do. And don't ever forget: There is nothing stronger than the power of **true friendship**!

And that's the truth — mouse's honor!

ABOUT THE AUTHOR

Born in New Mouse City, Mouse Island, **GERONIMO STILTON** is Rattus Emeritus of Mousomorphic Literature and of Neo-Ratonic Comparative Philosophy. For the past twenty years, he has been running *The Rodent's Gazette*, New Mouse City's most widely read daily newspaper.

Stilton was awarded the Ratitzer Prize for his scoops on *The Curse of the Cheese Pyramid* and *The Search for Sunken Treasure*. He has also received the Andersen 2000 Prize for Personality of the Year. One of his bestsellers won the 2002 eBook Award for world's best ratling's electronic book. His works have been published all over the globe.

In his spare time, Mr. Stilton collects antique cheese rinds and plays golf. But what he most enjoys is telling stories to his nephew Benjamin.

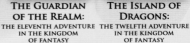

Don't miss any of my adventures in the Kingdom of Fantasy!

THE KINGDOM OF FANTASY

THE QUEST FOR PARADISE:
THE RETURN TO THE KINGDOM OF FANTASY

THE AMAZING VOYAGE:
THE THIRD ADVENTURE IN THE KINGDOM OF FANTASY

THE DRAGON PROPHECY:
THE FOURTH ADVENTURE IN THE KINGDOM OF FANTASY

THE VOLCANO OF FIRE:
THE FIFTH ADVENTURE IN THE KINGDOM OF FANTASY

THE SEARCH FOR TREASURE:
THE SIXTH ADVENTURE IN THE KINGDOM OF FANTASY

THE ENCHANTED CHARMS:
THE SEVENTH ADVENTURE IN THE KINGDOM OF FANTASY

THE PHOENIX OF DESTINY:
AN EPIC KINGDOM OF FANTASY ADVENTURE

THE HOUR OF MAGIC:
THE EIGHTH ADVENTURE IN THE KINGDOM OF FANTASY

THE WIZARD'S WAND:
THE NINTH ADVENTURE IN THE KINGDOM OF FANTASY

THE SHIP OF SECRETS:
THE TENTH ADVENTURE IN THE KINGDOM OF FANTASY

THE DRAGON OF FORTUNE:
AN EPIC KINGDOM OF FANTASY ADVENTURE

THE GUARDIAN OF THE REALM:
THE ELEVENTH ADVENTURE IN THE KINGDOM OF FANTASY

THE ISLAND OF DRAGONS:
THE TWELFTH ADVENTURE IN THE KINGDOM OF FANTASY

Don't miss a single fabumouse adventure!